*"The most important thing my mama taught us was
that God loves us and has a plan for our lives that goes
far beyond slavery or prejudice."*

—BESSIE GOODMAN, 1871

Savannah Secrets

Savannah Secrets

True Grits

NANCY MEHL

Guideposts

Danbury, Connecticut

Cover and interior design by Müllerhaus
Cover illustration by Pierre Droal, represented by Deborah Wolfe, LTD.
Typeset by Aptara, Inc.

Printed and bound in the United States of America
10 9 8 7 6 5 4 3 2 1

True Grits

Chapter One

June 1871

"Mama, what's for supper?" Bessie asked. "Me and Joseph are real hungry."

Portia smiled at her. "I'm not so sure you're thinkin' 'bout your brother. I think you're thinkin' 'bout yourself."

Bessie smiled. "You're the best cook in Savannah, Mama. We need to write down your recipes so we can keep 'em safe. Mother Mathilda says keepin' a history of who we is...I mean, who we are...is important."

"You know I can't write, Bessie. I know how to make things by keepin' the ingredients in my head. I don't need to write 'em down."

"But I can write. If you tell me 'bout how you make your good dishes, I can put it down on paper. Then we can put all the papers together. It will be like...a book."

Portia stirred the pot of grits on her woodburning stove. "I don't know. You have to be quiet 'bout school and stuff. You know we can get Mother Mathilda in a lot of trouble. She's not supposed to be teachin' Black children."

"I won't tell nobody—I mean anybody—'bout it. Please. I think Mother Mathilda would be pleased."

"I don't know…."

"Mama, did you make up how to fix grits?" Bessie asked.

"No, child," she answered. "We learned it from the Indians."

Bessie's eyes grew wide. "The Indians?"

"Yes, ma'am. But we done changed the recipe some from the way the Native people did theirs."

"I love it. It's my favorite food in the whole world."

Portia laughed. "You say everything is your favorite food. You go call Joseph in for supper. We're havin' ham hocks too. I know you like 'em."

Bessie smiled. "Okay. Will Papa be home for supper?"

Portia shook her head. "Farmer Johnson won't let him off until all the work is done. I'll keep some food warm on the stove."

"All right." Bessie started toward the front door of their small log cabin. Then she turned around. "I truly want to write down your recipes, Mama. Please. I think it's important."

Portia made a clucking sound with her tongue. "All right, Bessie Mae. We'll talk 'bout it later. Get your brother."

Portia was happy Bessie was learning things she herself had never had the chance to learn. She respected Mathilda Beasley more than any Black woman she'd ever met. Mother Mathilda, as she was called, taught a small, secret school for Black children, even though it was against the law in Savannah.

Several other people did it too, knowing they could get in trouble if they were caught. White teachers would be fined five hundred dollars, more money than Portia could even imagine. Black teachers were fined one hundred dollars and could get up to thirty-two lashes in the public square. Yet the schools continued. It was a well-known secret.

Even though Portia and her husband had been given their freedom, she worried about Bessie and Joseph. Many Black people were still living as slaves. Some of her friends said that someday things would change for the better, but so far Portia wasn't seeing as much difference as she'd hoped for. Maybe someday...

"Are you ready yet?"

Julia Foley looked up to see her partner in Magnolia Investigations, Meredith Bellefontaine, standing in the doorway of her office.

"Just a minute," Julia said. "I'm trying to wrap up our last case."

Meredith stepped inside and frowned at her. "Are you talking about that stolen diamond necklace?"

Julia nodded.

"What is there to wrap up? We found the necklace hidden under the floorboards in the client's house. They were trying to bilk the insurance company out of thousands of dollars."

"Meredith, I remember what happened. I'm not senile, thank you. I just want to make sure I've noted everything in their file." She wrote something down and then closed the folder. "See? That didn't take that long."

Meredith sighed. "I guess. I want to get a spot up close. I really hope Charlene wins. Her shrimp and grits are incredible."

"Well, she made it this far. Down to the final five contestants."

Meredith pushed back a lock of blond hair that had fallen over her forehead. Julia could see that she was really nervous about the grits contest.

Charlene, the daughter of one of their dearest friends, Maggie Lu King, had a good chance of winning. She and over twenty other restaurant owners in Savannah had created the new event called True Grits. The winner of the True Grits Award would be featured in the *Savannah Tribune*. It should bring in a lot of new customers.

"I'm surprised Sally and Laurel are in the finals," Meredith said. "I thought they'd kill each other before the contest was over."

Sally Becker, the owner of Savannah Sally's, and Laurel Hurst, from Mama Louise's Kitchen, seemed to be taking the competition a little too seriously. Their bickering was a distraction to the other contestants. Julia hoped their adversarial attitudes wouldn't flair tonight and put a damper on the contest.

The judges overseeing the contest had warned them more than once. Each judge had been picked because of their connection to the culinary world in Savannah. Ernie Prothro, the food editor for the *Tribune*, was attending, as was Adelaide Bridges from *Southern Eats* magazine. The third judge was a woman with a cooking show on Channel 6. Beverly Innes was known for specializing in Southern cuisine. Three local news stations planned to show up and broadcast from the contest. More great exposure for Charlene and her Downhome Diner.

The event was being held on River Street, a beautiful area popular with tourists and residents alike. Thankfully, the weather was perfect. Seventy degrees in October.

Julia closed her laptop and grabbed her light jacket from the coatrack in her office. It would be chillier near the water, and she didn't want to be cold.

"You won't need that," Meredith said. "It's gorgeous outside."

"Easy for you to say since you keep your office like a meat locker."

"Oh, Julia," Meredith said, laughing. "I do not. I guess I'm just warm-blooded. I like my office…cool."

"Yeah," Julia mumbled. "I could keep ice cream in there."

Meredith giggled. "Come on. Let's go."

After they left out the back door of the old home that had been converted into Magnolia Investigations, Julia made sure the door was locked. Their assistant, Carmen Lopez, had already left for the weekend.

"I hope Carmen shows up," Meredith said.

"I do too. I think she'd enjoy it."

They got into Meredith's car and drove to River Street. Finding a place to park wasn't easy on a Friday night, but as Meredith searched for something, a car began to pull out of a space right in front of her.

"Hallelujah," she said. "I take this as a blessing. I'm wearing heels. I didn't want to have to walk too far."

Julia got out of the car and grabbed her wallet. "Okay. Let's go," she said.

Meredith locked the car. "I really want Charlene to win."

"I do too, but we'll enjoy it no matter what happens. At least she made it through three rounds. She has a good chance."

Meredith took a deep breath and blew it out. "You're right."

They walked down River Street, next to the Savannah River. The setting sun splashed red and orange on the water, making it sparkle like fire. It was so beautiful, Julia stopped for a moment to take it in.

"Let's go," Meredith said, pulling on her arm.

"All right. I just love River Street."

"It is special, isn't it?"

Julia drank in the splendor once more before hurrying toward the spot that had been set up for the competition. The contestants were busy preparing their dishes using hot plates and steam trays. Each contestant was supposed to present three bowls of grits. Each bowl had a number written on the side that corresponded to the judge. Presentation was also important, so each chef worked hard to make their dish look appealing.

Julia and Meredith tried to get as close as they could to the long tables that were pushed together where the chefs worked. Charlene's cook, Maribelle Sims, was busy preparing her signature shrimp and grits. The dish was well known in Savannah and other restaurants served it, but no one made it taste the way Maribelle did.

Julia saw Charlene and Maggie Lu, standing off to the side. Charlene looked nervous, but Maggie Lu seemed calm and unflustered by what was going on.

Julia caught Maggie Lu's eye, and she grinned at them.

"This is nerve racking," Meredith said. "I could never do something like this."

"You can do anything you want," Julia said with a smile. "You're a great baker. You could win a contest, you know."

Meredith laughed. "Maybe, but right now I'm busy enough working cases with you."

Julia smiled. "Good point."

Someone tapped Julia's shoulder, and she turned around to see Carmen. "There you are," Julia said. "It's almost time."

Carmen held up a to-go cup. "I know, but I needed a Mucho Mocha from A Cup of Jo."

The small café on River Street, run by Jo McAllister, was a favorite of tourists and locals. Most of the coffee shops were closed in the evening, but Jo kept hers open until ten to catch the strollers who loved coffee any time of the day.

A bell rang, and the women looked toward the tables. Time for the judges. Julia glanced over at Maggie Lu. Still cool, but she noticed that Charlene had reached for her mother's hand.

"Good evening, ladies and gentlemen." The announcer for the evening, Barbie Patzweaver, host of a local morning show on Channel 4 in Savannah, flashed her familiar smile at the assembled crowd. "We are ready for the judging." She turned to the contestants. "Please step back from the table and from your dishes." She used her free hand to smooth her hair where the breeze had ruffled it.

"Each chef has prepared three bowls of grits for the judges to taste. When a judge tries one dish, he or she will be given time to make notes in the scoring notebook before moving on to the next offering. Once they have tried all five samples, they will be given fifteen minutes to fill out a scorecard for each restaurant. Then the cards will be turned in to our head judge, Mr. Ernie Prothro, from the *Savannah Tribune*. He will add up the scores and announce our winner."

She paused for a moment to allow spectators to clap. When no one did, she began to do so while holding the microphone. Each time she clapped, there was a loud thud, making several in the crowd jump.

After a few tepid claps from the crowd, she walked in front of the long table. "It is my honor to introduce each restaurant and chef represented here tonight."

"The food's gonna be cold by the time she gets through strutting around," Carmen said under her breath. Unfortunately, an older couple standing nearby overheard and glared at her.

"Contestant number one is Martin Seeger from the Seaside Grill." A few shouts erupted from the crowd. "Contestant number two is Sally

Becker from Savannah Sally's. Contestant three is Jerome Matheson, chef from Mama Louise's Kitchen, owned by Laurel Hurst."

The older couple who had shot them dirty looks earlier yelled their enthusiasm for Laurel.

"Contestant four is Maribelle Sims, cook from the Downhome Diner, owned by Charlene Jackson."

Julia, Meredith, and Carmen hollered their support for Charlene.

"And finally, we welcome Cyrus Sharrah from Sharrah's on River Street."

There was a smattering of applause for Cyrus.

"And now, would our chefs have a seat while the judges take their places?" Barbie said with another big smile. Her teeth were so white that Julia couldn't help but wonder what she used to get them like that.

"Our judges tonight are from some of Savannah's most prestigious restaurants. So our dishes don't get cold, we'll introduce them later, when they share their scores. When I ring this bell, judges, please taste the dish in front of you. When I ring it again, please move down the line to the next. You will have ninety seconds to taste and make notes before I ring the bell again for you to move to the next dish. When you're done, you may sit down and fill out your final scorecard." Another flash of teeth. Then she rang the bell.

Barbie was standing at the end of the table, next to the dish made by Cyrus. With her smile intact, Barbie watched as Beverly Innes tasted his grits and cheese, turned dark red, and promptly threw up all over Barbie's nice white pantsuit.

Chapter Two

THE CROWD SEEMED FROZEN IN place. Everyone was apparently shocked into silence except for Carmen, who loudly exclaimed, "¡Ay, caramba!"

It was evident very quickly that Beverly wasn't the only one in distress. Ernie Prothro fainted and fell to the ground. People began calling for a doctor. Thankfully, two were in the crowd.

"Call 911!" one of them yelled.

Shocked by what had happened, Julia just stood where she was, not sure what to do. It was then that she realized that Adelaide Bridges appeared to be fine after trying Maribelle's shrimp and grits. Although Adelaide didn't look sick, she seemed very concerned, as if she was waiting for the same malady that had seized her colleagues to overtake her as well.

"Let's step back and give the doctors some room," a man said.

Some people got up and hurried away as if afraid the judges had just contracted something deadly that could infect them as well.

"What can we do?" Julia asked Meredith.

"Nothing. Doctors are there and 911 has been contacted." Meredith shrugged. "Maybe we should just leave."

Julia waved her hand. "Just a minute. I want to check on Maggie Lu and Charlene."

She pushed her way through the crowd until she was next to Maggie Lu. "Are you all right?" she asked.

Maggie Lu took her arm. "I have no earthly idea what's happening," she said. "What could have made those poor judges so sick?"

"The judge that tasted our grits seems to be okay," Charlene added.

"Well, thank God for small favors."

Julia turned around to find that Meredith had followed her. She smiled at her. "I agree," Julia said. "But…"

"But it doesn't look good for us?" Maggie Lu added. "You're right."

"I don't understand," Charlene said, frowning. "Why would…" Her eyes suddenly widened. "You mean people might think we have something to do with this? That we…we poisoned the other dishes?" She turned to look at Julia. "Surely no one would actually believe that we would poison everyone's food but ours."

Maribelle came hurrying up to Charlene. "I don't understand what's going on," she said. "But could it have anything to do with this paprika?" She held up a small jar.

"Can I see that?" Julia asked.

Maribelle nodded and handed her the jar. The label said it was paprika. The spice was used frequently with grits, not only in the recipe but also applied to the top of the dish. The paprika gave it a nice splash of color without changing the taste of the dish.

"I think everyone except me used it," Maribelle said in a whisper. "We use a special smoked paprika. It was inspired by Clementine's spice mixture."

Clementine had been married to Maggie Lu's brother, Benny. Just before she died, many years ago, she'd given Maggie Lu's grandmother an old book of recipes that had been passed down through her family.

Julia removed the cap from the jar and put it near her nose. She started to sniff the ingredients when she was seized by an overwhelming urge to sneeze. She touched some of the powder with her finger. Her skin immediately began to burn.

She grabbed a bottle of water from the table and poured some over her finger. "This isn't paprika," she said. "I'm not sure, but I think it might be ground ghost peppers. I tasted a dish made with them once. Horribly hot."

"Ghost peppers?" Carmen asked, her eyes wide. "My cousin Julio got really sick from eating those things."

Meredith frowned. "How could they have used it without knowing what it was? Smoked paprika and ghost peppers wouldn't smell anything alike. Wouldn't they have had the same reaction Julia just did?"

"Not necessarily," Julia said. "If you remember, the chefs were rushing toward the end and barely had time to shake this stuff on their grits. I heard Sally telling Martin to hurry up and give it to her."

"What should we do?" Charlene asked. "Don't we need to tell the police what we've found?"

Julia was just about to answer when several police cars pulled up near the contest area. Officers jumped out and began to question people. An ambulance came from the other direction and EMTs got out, looking for those suffering from the pepper.

"Give the jar to me," Meredith said. "I'll stick it in my purse. Then tomorrow we'll take it to the police station and tell them what happened."

"If we do that, it'll look like we're trying to get away with something," Julia said. "We need to put this back where Maribelle found it. It's evidence."

A shrill whine rose over the sound of the crowd. Julia looked toward the contest area and saw Barbie wailing over the mess on her pantsuit. Her cameraman was obviously trying to appease her, but personalities from other TV stations seemed to be rather amused by the poor woman's predicament.

Maribelle grabbed the jar from Julia's hand and said, "Just give it to me. I caused this mess, and I'm gonna fix it." Maribelle was a stout woman, probably in her late fifties, and she was a force to be reckoned with. Julia would love to have just a small amount of her energy.

Maribelle hurried over to her cooking equipment on the table and seemed to be turning off her hot plate, but Julia saw her remove the jar from her pocket and quickly slip it onto the table. Thankfully, it didn't seem that anyone was paying attention to her. The crowd was focused on the four or five other police cruisers arriving on the scene. It certainly seemed like overkill for two people who had eaten an overly hot spice.

A police officer walked up to the front and faced the crowd. One of the news reporters handed him a microphone.

"Ladies and gentlemen, we're asking that you leave this area unless you're directly connected to the contestants or judges, or you have knowledge as to what happened."

People began to slowly drift away.

"We need to go," Meredith said to Julia.

"Call us," Julia told Maggie Lu and Charlene. "Let us know that everything's okay."

"I'm so grateful Maribelle didn't use that spice," Charlene said in a low voice. "If we didn't have our own smoked paprika, she probably would have used some from that jar too."

"Just make sure you show the police that you brought your own spice if they question you," Julia said.

"You think they might suspect us, don't you?" Charlene asked.

"Actually, no. No one with any sense would let competitors sprinkle ghost pepper on their food. Now if it was simply something that tasted bad, that's one thing. But why would anyone sabotage an opponent with something so obviously suspect?"

"I guess so," Charlene said slowly.

"It'll be fine," Meredith said. "Just tell the truth. You have nothing to be concerned about."

"You're right," Maggie Lu said, a smile on her face. "I'm sure everything will be okay. You go on home. I'll check in with you tomorrow."

"All right." Julia didn't feel good about leaving their friends behind, but they had to obey the police. She completely understood why they were asking people to leave.

Suddenly another ambulance pulled up. She wondered why. Ernie was inside the first ambulance and Beverly Innes, the judge who threw up on Barbie, seemed to be doing much better.

Poor Barbie was still upset about her pantsuit. One of her camera people was asking her to go on air and make a report.

"How can I do that?" she cried. "I'm a ruined mess. I need to go home and change. Right now!"

A nearby police officer rolled his eyes and said something to a fellow officer who appeared to be trying to appease the agitated news anchor.

Julia shook her head. "I'll never see her the same way again."

"I guess I'll head home," Carmen said. "This wasn't what I expected. But thanks for asking me. It was…interesting."

Julia laughed. "Sorry. We had no idea it was going to turn out this way. If you're not doing anything, let's get some supper. We've got a lot of restaurants to choose from."

Before Carmen had a chance to respond, her phone rang. She'd set her ringtone to "*La Cucaracha*," which always made Julia laugh. Carmen looked at the display, and her cheeks reddened. She held up one finger and walked away to take the call.

"I have a feeling we just lost our dinner pal," Julia said with a smile.

Meredith laughed. "I think you're right. I asked Chase if he wanted to come to the contest tonight, and he turned me down. I think I know why."

The women waited until Carmen came back. "I'm sorry," she said. "It seems I have other plans tonight."

Meredith smiled at her. "We'll see you Monday morning."

"*Sí*," Carmen said.

"Have a good time," Meredith said.

Carmen grinned. "I will. *Gracias*."

She turned and hurried away.

"I wonder if she's off to see Chase," Meredith mused. "Do you need to go home to Beau?"

"Not tonight," Julia said, putting her arm through Meredith's. "I told him this evening would be spent with my best friend. Let's get something to eat. I'm starving."

"After watching that fiasco?" Meredith asked. "How could you be hungry?"

"I don't know. I just am."

Meredith grinned. "Okay, if you can eat after that, I guess I can too. But let's not go anywhere that uses ghost peppers."

"Agreed."

"Or serves grits."

Julia laughed. "Also agreed."

The women waved goodbye to Maggie Lu and Charlene and walked away from the contest area. A man who was looking the other way turned quickly and ran right into Julia. If Meredith hadn't grabbed her by the arm, he could have knocked her over.

"I'm so sorry," he said. "I wasn't watching where I was going. Are you all right?"

"Yes, I think so," Julia said. "Guess we need stoplights on River Street."

The man laughed. "That might be true. Again, I'm terribly sorry. Glad you're okay."

"Thank you."

"Let's find a restaurant before something else happens," Meredith said.

"Yes, please. I've had enough for one night."

A short time later they were sitting at a table in a popular steak restaurant, looking out over the water. Their meals were perfect. Meredith had steak with Gorgonzola sauce, and Julia ordered herb-crusted filet mignon.

Meredith sighed with contentment after swallowing her last bite. "This night started off badly, but it's much better now. Thanks, Julia."

"Dessert?" Julia asked.

"Couldn't possibly. I'm stuffed. But you go ahead."

"I think I'm done too. I couldn't eat another bite."

Meredith reached for the bill the waiter had left on the table.

"I want to get this," Julia said. "I think you picked up the tab last time." She put her hand into her jacket pocket for her wallet and felt her stomach turn over. She quickly checked her other pockets.

"What's wrong?" Meredith asked.

"My wallet. Meredith, it's gone."

Chapter Three

THE WOMEN WAITED AT A table on River Street for the police to arrive. Julia was distraught.

"It was that man who ran into me," she said. "I should have known. It's a trick pickpockets use all the time. Why didn't I realize it?"

"I didn't catch it either," Meredith said.

"I should have been suspicious when it happened. I was thinking about Charlene and not paying attention. Thankfully, I have a company that protects my credit cards. I need to call them right away."

Meredith waited while Julia made her call. A few minutes later, she hung up. "The thief already tried to use one of my cards. Two thousand dollars at Mr. Andre's."

Mr. Andre's was a high-dollar men's clothing store in Savannah.

"They refused to honor it and called me to ask about it. I forgot to turn my ringer back on after the contest, so I missed their call."

"So he didn't get away with his purchase?" Meredith asked.

Julia shook her head. "Thankfully, no. The card protection company will take care of canceling all my credit cards so the thief won't be able to use any of them."

"Did you have any cash in your wallet?" Meredith asked.

Julia nodded. "Some." Her eyes filled with tears. "I don't care about that. I don't even care about the credit cards."

"Then what's wrong?"

"I had a picture of my father in my wallet." Julia's father had been killed in a car accident in 2005.

"Jules, you have lots of pictures of your father. Is there something special about that picture?"

Julia took a deep, shuddering breath. "Yes, it was taken the day before he was killed. My mom took a picture of us together. It's…it's the way I remember him. There was also a letter he wrote to me after I passed the bar, telling me how proud he was of me. It's not that I can't remember what it said. I memorized it a long time ago."

"But it was in his handwriting?"

Julia nodded.

"Don't worry. You know the thief will probably toss the wallet. I'll bet someone will find it and call you. It's happened before."

Julia wiped away a tear. "It's possible. I shouldn't get so emotional. It's just…sometimes I miss my dad. He was a wonderful father."

"Let's not give up, okay? We'll find the guy who took your wallet. I mean, that's what we do, right?"

"I guess."

A police car pulled up next to the restaurant. The women waved him over.

"Did you call about a stolen wallet?" he asked after he got out of the car.

"Yes," Julia said.

The officer sat down, and Julia began to tell him about the man who ran into her and what was in her wallet.

"Can you describe him?" the officer asked.

Julia tried her best to remember what he looked like. "To be honest, he almost knocked me off my feet. I was concentrating on not falling down. I didn't get a good look at him."

"I saw him," Meredith said.

As Meredith described the man to the officer, Julia's mind turned to what Meredith had said about finding the wallet. Yes, sometimes they were returned by people who discovered them tossed on the ground somewhere, but many times they were put into dumpsters and never seen again. She prayed that wouldn't happen this time.

**

Julia and Beau spent a quiet weekend at home, except for church Sunday morning. Julia loved their church, New Beginnings. She also enjoyed volunteering as a leader in the youth group on Wednesday nights.

After church they picked up lunch from Peachie's, one of Julia's favorite restaurants. The cheeseburgers were out of this world, and the milkshakes were scrumptious. Since it was October, Julia had a pumpkin spice shake. Beau was a milkshake purist and only went for chocolate, strawberry, or vanilla. Today it was chocolate.

He was upset that someone had taken her wallet but was very relieved no one would be using the credit cards. He listened as she talked about the picture and the letter and tried to reassure her just as Meredith had. Their encouragement kept her feeling hopeful that she just might get her picture and letter back.

After eating, Beau put his feet up on the couch to read the Sunday newspaper. It was the only print copy they got during the week. Within a few minutes, he was asleep—his regular Sunday routine.

Julia was in the kitchen when the phone rang. It was Meredith, asking if she'd heard anything from the police.

"Not a thing." She sighed. "I keep hoping they'll call."

"Don't give up," Meredith said. "When we get into the office tomorrow, we'll come up with a more accurate description of the thief. Maybe we can even draw a picture of him. It might help."

"Not if I draw it," Julia said. "I don't think the police are into searching for stick figures."

Meredith laughed. "Hey, Carmen can draw. I've seen some of her sketches. She hides them in her notebooks. I'm sure she'd be willing to help."

"Yeah, maybe."

"So what are you and Beau doing today?"

"Absolutely nothing. We went to church then picked up food from Peachies. Beau's snoring on the couch. I've been wanting to clean out the refrigerator. This is a good day to do it."

Meredith sighed. "You would mention your refrigerator. I need to clean mine too. I've been ignoring it for too long. There's *something* in a plastic storage container in the back. It's been there so long I can't remember what it is."

"I've got a couple of those. I'm kind of afraid to know what's inside. I may just throw them out without even looking."

Meredith laughed again. "Be brave. By the end of the day we'll both have clean fridges."

"Sounds good."

"So are you doing okay, Jules?"

"Not really. One voice in my head tells me I'm being silly over an old photo and a piece of paper. But another voice says that these things represented a special memory. I feel violated that someone took them from me."

"Of course you do," Meredith said. "Anyone would."

"Well, thanks for checking on me. If I hear anything from the police, I'll let you know." Julia paused. "Have you talked to Charlene or Maggie Lu today?"

"Not yet, but I plan to call Maggie Lu this afternoon if I don't hear from her soon."

"Weird how everyone got sick at the contest except the judge who tasted grits from the Downhome Diner," Julia said.

"Yeah, and that still makes me a little nervous."

"Because you wonder if people will blame Charlene for what happened?"

"Exactly. I mean, we know she didn't do anything wrong, but other people don't know Charlene the way we do."

"Yeah. Hey, call me after you talk to Maggie Lu, okay?" Julia asked. "Let me know if there's anything I can do to help."

"I will."

"Have a good afternoon, Mere. And give GK a kiss for me." GK was Meredith's gorgeous Russian blue cat.

"If you hug Bunny for me."

"I'll try, but she only allows hugs if she's in the mood for them."

Meredith chuckled and said goodbye.

Julia stared at her phone for a while after Meredith hung up. She really was worried. She knew without a doubt Charlene was innocent. Surely no one could believe that she had anything to do with what happened at the contest.

Could they?

Chapter Four

Julia arrived at the office a little early. She'd stopped by Etienne's, a favorite bakery nearby, to pick up beignets.

"*Muy bien*," Carmen said when she saw the box in Julia's hands. "Do you want me to take the box back to the conference room?"

"Thank you," Julia said. "I appreciate it."

Julia handed the box to Carmen and went to her office. She loved its charm and elegance. Rich wood panels covered the walls from floor to ceiling. A large white fireplace dominated one wall, and a gilded mirror hung above the mantel. Seafoam-green drapes matched the needlepoint on the cushions of her two carved French Louis XV chairs. The rest of the office was decorated in soft gray tones. An Aubusson rug finished off the chic room.

She hung up her jacket and put her purse in the bottom drawer of her desk. She was just getting ready to grab some coffee and head to the conference room when Carmen walked in.

"We have guests," she said.

Julia frowned at her. There were no appointments scheduled for this morning. "Who?"

Before Carmen had a chance to answer, Maggie Lu slid past her and rushed toward Julia's desk.

"You've got to help," she said.

Julia could see the stress in her friend's face. "Sit down and tell me what's wrong," she said. She gestured toward one of the chairs in front of her desk. "Coffee?" she asked.

"Yes, please."

Julia nodded at Carmen, who quietly closed the office door. It was only shut a few seconds when it opened again. Meredith came in and sat down next to Maggie Lu. She'd tried to reach Maggie Lu the night before, even left a message, but hadn't heard back. She'd called Julia to let her know. They'd both been worried.

"What's wrong?" Julia asked.

"The police think Charlene had something to do with what happened Friday night," Maggie Lu said. "Now you both know Charlene well enough to know that's not possible. Charlene is as honest as the day is long. She would never, ever cheat to win a contest. And the idea that she would intentionally harm someone?" Maggie Lu snorted. "Heavens to Betsy. Have you ever heard anything so ridiculous?"

"Slow down," Julia said. "What exactly do the police suspect Charlene of doing?"

Maggie Lu sighed. "She was called down to the station this morning. They asked her why everyone else's grits were tainted except hers. As if Charlene would know the answer."

"Did they figure out what was in that jar?" Meredith asked.

Maggie Lu's face knotted in a deep frown. "Julia was right. Ground ghost pepper. My goodness gracious. I sure wish Maribelle hadn't taken that jar from the table. What if someone saw her?" She shook her head. "Mercy me, what a mess."

The door opened, and Carmen came in carrying a tray with coffee and condiments.

"So they're absolutely certain that's what was in the jar?" Meredith asked.

"Yes. Seems everyone except Maribelle used it to give their grits color. That's what those poor judges ate. Ernie Prothro is still in the hospital. They say he'll be okay, but he took a big bite that had been covered with that stuff."

"Whose dish did he taste?"

"I believe it was the one from Mama Louise's."

Everyone took a cup of coffee, and Julia thanked Carmen, who smiled and slipped out the door, closing it behind her.

"So the police think Charlene put that jar on the table, hoping the other contestants would use it?" Julia asked.

"I suppose so," Maggie Lu answered.

"They're not charging her with anything, are they?"

Maggie Lu shook her head. "No, not yet. They don't have any proof. But it's pretty clear that they suspect her. Seems the other contestants do too."

"How do you know that?" Meredith asked.

"From something the police said, I guess. She's really worried." Maggie Lu fastened her gaze on Julia and Meredith. "That's why we want to hire you."

"Hire us?" Julia asked. "For what?"

"To defend my Charlene. And to find out who really did this. It's the only way to clear her name." She looked back and forth between Julia and Meredith. "Of course, we'll pay you."

"Oh, Maggie Lu, don't be silly," Meredith said. "Of course you won't pay us. My goodness, I can't even count how many times you've helped us solve cases. We'd be happy to check it out. We'll need to speak to Charlene. Can she come by here this afternoon? And we need to talk to Maribelle too."

"I'll call Charlene in a bit and tell her. She'll need to get people to cover for her and Maribelle."

Carmen opened the door to the office and stepped inside, holding a newspaper. "I'm sorry to interrupt you, but you need to see this. A friend of mine dropped it off." She put the paper on Julia's desk. The Saturday *Savannah Tribune* had splashed a picture taken at the contest on the front page. It read LOCAL COOKING CONTEST SENDS JUDGES TO THE HOSPITAL.

Julia picked up the paper and read, "'Friday night on River Street, people gathered to watch a showdown between several of Savannah's popular restaurants. The contest, called True Grits, highlighted the city's best grits recipes. Unfortunately, someone decided to add a special ingredient, and several of the competition's judges got more than they bargained for. It appears that someone spiked the grits with some kind of hot pepper. One judge was treated at the scene and released. But Ernie Prothro, our culinary editor, was taken to the hospital, where he is recovering. Bystanders say that only one of the entries wasn't treated with the pepper. Mr. Prothro wonders why the Downhome Diner escaped the attack and suggests that it may have been an irresponsible attempt to win the competition. He is planning to file a lawsuit, charging the Downhome Diner with reckless endangerment. The police are investigating. We will certainly continue to follow this story. Hopefully, the truth will be uncovered soon.'" Julia looked up at Maggie Lu, who seemed shocked by what she'd heard.

Maggie Lu's eyes filled with tears. "People are going to believe my Charlene had something to do with what happened. This is just terrible." She rose to her feet. "Please, we have to fix this!"

"Don't worry, Maggie Lu," Meredith said soothingly. "We'll get to the bottom of it. Everything will be okay."

Maggie Lu pulled a tissue out of her purse. "I'd better get to Charlene. She hasn't seen this. When she hears about it…" She wiped away the tears on her cheeks. Then she pasted a smile on her face. "Can't let her think her mama is worried. Nothing bothers a child more than seeing her mama afraid."

Meredith stood up and gave Maggie Lu a hug. After promising she'd send Charlene and Maribelle down to the office, Maggie Lu left.

"Oh, Julia," Meredith said. "Who would do something like this?"

"I don't know, but we need to make a list of everyone involved with the contest. Start going through every contestant, every judge…" Julia looked at the clock on the wall. "But before we do that, can we grab Carmen and go to the conference room? See if she can draw a picture of the guy who took my wallet. I'd like to get this out of the way before we get entrenched in Charlene's situation. I can't get it out of my head."

Meredith stood up. "Okay. I'll get her."

Julia took her coffee and headed to the conference room. She sat down at the gorgeous rosewood table. The room was once Ron's office, but when Meredith was ready to move his things out, they'd redone the room. It was lovely now. The walls were papered in yellow silk and at the windows were soft white wooden shutters. A large crystal chandelier hung from the ceiling above them. Boston ferns on antique iron plant stands stood in front of the windows.

Julia opened the box from Etienne's. Then she got some paper plates, napkins, and forks from a nearby cabinet. By the time Meredith and Carmen arrived she had everything ready.

"Etienne's," Meredith said with a smile. "I kept thinking I smelled beignets but had decided it must be my imagination." She sat down next to Julia.

Julia laughed. "No, it was real. They won't be warm anymore though."

"Give me that box," Carmen said. "I'll nuke them just a touch."

"Thank you, Carmen," Julia said.

When Carmen left the room, Meredith leaned closer to Julia. "Carmen didn't want to do this," she said in a low voice. "She doesn't think she draws well. I had to almost beg her to help us."

"But you said you've seen some of her sketches?"

Meredith nodded. "She's good. She's just not confident."

Carmen walked through the door and the scent of beignets filled the room. She put the box on the table then reached in and took out two containers.

"I asked for raspberry and dark chocolate espresso sauce," Julia said.

Meredith smiled. "Perfect."

"*Muy bien*," Carmen said.

Julia knew Carmen was a fan of the dark chocolate espresso. It really was delicious.

Once they'd each fixed their plates, Julia told Carmen about the theft on Friday night.

"Meredith mentioned it," Carmen said after swallowing a bite of her pastry. "You have that service, right? The one that takes care of your credit cards if they're stolen?"

"Yes, thankfully."

Carmen frowned. "So you need to get your IDs back?"

"I carry my driver's license in my phone wallet," Julia said. "That, and an emergency twenty-dollar bill. That way if I go out for a walk I just grab my phone instead of having to carry a purse,"

"That's fantastic," Meredith said. "One less thing to replace."

Julia nodded.

"I don't understand," Carmen said, her expression showing her confusion. "Why is it so important to find this man? I mean, the money is a concern, but you probably won't get that back."

Julia took a deep breath and told Carmen about the picture and the letter. By the time she finished, Carmen's eyes were filled with sympathy.

"We will find this *villano*." She took out her sketch pad. "Can you tell me what he looked like?" she asked Julia.

"To be honest, I didn't see him clearly," she said. "I was trying to stay on my feet. He hit me pretty hard. You said you got a clear look at him, Meredith?"

Meredith nodded. "I was so surprised when he ran into you that I looked directly at him. I'm sure I can give you a good idea of what he looks like, Carmen."

Julia sipped her coffee while the two women worked on the sketch. Before long a face appeared.

"And he had a scar," Meredith said. She pointed to his cheek. "Right here. Crescent shaped."

Julia gasped. "I wasn't listening to you when you talked to the police. If I had... If I'd known about the scar..."

"What's wrong?" Meredith asked.

Julia pulled the sketchbook toward herself, trying to grasp what she was seeing. She pointed at the picture. "I recognize this man. I know who he is."

Chapter Five

MEREDITH AND CARMEN STARED AT her in surprise.

"What do you mean, you know him?" Meredith asked.

Julia took a sip of coffee, trying to calm down before saying, "I should have said I *knew* him. His name is Grady Prescott." She was quiet for a moment. "Goodness, he must be almost forty by now. He was in his twenties when I dealt with him."

"What did he do?" Meredith asked.

"Two counts of armed robbery. Under Georgia law, he received life in prison without the possibility of parole." She picked up her coffee cup again. "As you know, Georgia has some of the strictest sentencing guidelines in the country. For the 'Seven Deadly Sins' it's two strikes and you're out. Used to be that felons incarcerated before 1995 only served a third of their sentences. Then the federal government created VOTIS, the Violent Offender Incarceration Truth In Sentencing program. They give Georgia funds to help them build additional prison space for offenders so they aren't released too early."

Meredith stared at the face Carmen had drawn. "Are you sure this is him? I mean, from a sketch?"

"It's this." Julia pointed at the crescent-shaped scar on the man's cheek. "It's too much to believe that he looks so much like Prescott and has the same scar. This was my last case before I moved to

Savannah. There's no reason for him to be out. Like I said, parole wasn't possible for him."

"Is there someone you can call to see why this man is out?" Carmen asked.

"Yes, there is. I'll do that right now."

As she walked down the hall to her office, Julia turned Grady Prescott's case over in her mind. He'd been a troubled youth, in and out of the court system. When he became an adult, he continued his life of crime. First shoplifting, then stolen checks. He'd only been out of prison for a year when he robbed two senior citizens at night on the street. He'd pointed a gun at them and taken their money and their jewelry. Two days later he did the same thing to another elderly couple, except this time he pistol-whipped the seventy-year-old man when he refused to let Prescott take his wife's wedding ring.

The case was so clear in Julia's mind, not only because it was the last case she'd prosecuted before she became a judge but also because of the heinous nature of the crime. Another thing that stuck in her mind was Prescott's scar. It was the scar that had sealed his fate. Although the description the couples gave was a little shaky, they all mentioned the scar. When Prescott was found guilty, Julia didn't need to ask for the maximum sentence, because Georgia law had done it for her.

She sat down in her office chair, woke up her computer, and googled Sheila Alton, Deputy District Attorney for Fulton County. She placed the call and was surprised when she got a real live person.

"Sheila?" she said. "It's Julia Foley."

"Julia? It's been years. How are you? Are you still working in juvenile justice?"

"No, I've been retired for a while. You may not believe this, but I'm actually working for a private detective agency."

A warm chuckle came over the phone. "Actually, I can easily believe it. You have a strong desire to search for justice. I've always admired that about you."

"Thanks, Sheila. That means a lot. How are you doing?"

"Pretty good, maybe a little burned out. Retirement is looking pretty good. My daughter runs an animal rescue business. She asked me to work with her. I think I'll do it."

"You were always crazy about animals. I still remember Teddy, that darling mutt you rescued. Didn't you say the shelter didn't want to give him to you?"

Sheila was quiet for a moment. Finally, she said, "I had to sign a release form stating that I wouldn't hold them accountable for any injuries I received from him." Julia heard her sniff. "When I got him home, he wouldn't even look at me. He had wounds from someone throwing scalding liquid on his back."

"You certainly turned him around," Julia said gently.

"Yes, he became a cuddle bug. Followed me everywhere. Almost every picture I took of him shows him smiling."

"He was so blessed to have you in his life."

"He's been gone a while now. I miss him every day. My daughter's rescue business is called Teddy's Place." She cleared her throat. "I'm sure you have another reason for calling besides trying to make me cry." She chuckled again.

"I do. Do you remember Grady Prescott?"

"Absolutely."

"You might think I'm losing it, but I'm almost positive I saw him Friday night. In Savannah."

Sheila was so quiet, for a moment Julia thought they'd been disconnected.

"You certainly could have seen him, Julia. I have no idea why he's in Savannah though."

It took Julia a moment to recover from Sheila's affirmation of her sighting. "But he's supposed to be spending life in prison without the possibility of parole. So how could he be here?"

"He was granted a new trial. One of the original witnesses recanted his testimony."

"One of them?" Julia asked.

"Yes. Leo Moreland, the elderly man Prescott was alleged to have pistol-whipped?"

"Alleged to?" Julia asked. "Sheila, you know he did it. I just don't know what to say."

"Actually, the testimony was pretty convincing, Julia. Another man in prison admitted to committing both crimes."

"But our eyewitness testimony…"

"This man looks a lot like Prescott. And he has the same kind of scar."

"But why would this man confess? Won't that keep him in prison for the rest of his life?"

"Yes," Sheila said, "but he was scheduled for execution. He was offered a deal to come forward. Now the death penalty is off the table."

Julia felt a rush of anger. "The DA made this ridiculous deal?"

"Yes. Several of us spoke to him, but he's convinced Prescott is innocent of the armed robberies. After the trial he was granted a full pardon from the State Board of Pardons and Paroles, with a recommendation from the DA."

"Sheila, do you believe he was wrongly convicted?"

Shelia sighed. "I don't know, Julia. Like I said, the evidence is compelling. The inmate, Gerald Turano, was in the area on the dates in question. He was convicted of an earlier armed robbery that resulted in a death. During the new trial, the victim was unsure if his attacker was Prescott or Turano, but he leaned toward Turano. Turano even owned the type of gun used in the robberies. You remember that we never had fingerprints. Just the eyewitness testimony of the four victims."

"What about the other victims? Were they called in to testify?"

"It's been a while, Julia. They've all passed away." Another sigh. "Look, I'm not any happier than you are about this. If you say you saw him, you need to be careful. He could be targeting you. Tell the local police to keep an eye on him."

"I have no idea where he is now," Julia said. "But he knows how to find me. He stole my wallet. He tried to use one of my credit cards, but he was shut down through my credit card protection company."

"Julia, please be careful. I don't trust that guy."

"But why come after me? I had nothing to do with his sentence. And the judge had to follow the law."

"I know that," Sheila said, "but some people need to find others to blame for their own mistakes. We've seen it many times."

"If he was pardoned, then he has no parole officer?" Julia asked. "No one to be accountable to?"

"Right. He's free and clear. The court applied time served to his other convictions. He's been out almost nine months now."

After thanking Sheila for her help, Julia hung up. Her thoughts kept swinging back and forth between two possibilities. One was that she'd helped send an innocent man to prison. The guilt from that possibility weighed heavily on her.

The other possibility was that a very dangerous man was on the loose in Savannah, and he might be targeting her.

Right now she wasn't certain which prospect was worse.

Chapter Six

WHEN JULIA WENT BACK TO the conference room, Meredith and Carmen must have been able to see her distress.

"Julia, what's wrong?" Meredith asked.

"You look troubled," Carmen said.

She briefly told them about her conversation with Sheila.

"Oh, Julia," Meredith said. "We really should call the police."

"We did," Julia said. "They're looking for my wallet." She shook her head. "What if I was wrong, Meredith? What if Grady Prescott was innocent?"

"So you think his being in Savannah is a coincidence?"

"It could be."

"*Desperado,*" Carmen said under her breath.

The agency's phone rang from Carmen's desk. "You need to be careful," Carmen said, shaking her finger at Julia before grabbing her coffee and half-eaten beignet and hurrying off.

"Desperado indeed," Meredith said. "I don't like this, Julia." She frowned. "You may need to use that gun you carry."

"I haven't had it with me for a while," Julia said. "But I guess I'll start carrying it again. But you know, just because I carry a gun, it doesn't mean I ever want to shoot anyone. I hate the idea."

"I know that, Julia," Meredith said. "But you need to be safe. At least you know you're prepared if Prescott comes after you."

Julia clasped her hands. "Let's move on. I don't want to think about having to use my gun."

"Okay. You know, Julia, something's been bothering me about your wallet."

"What's that?"

"How did he know where it was?"

Julia stared at her. "You're right. He was watching us. Why didn't I realize that?"

"Because you were busy thinking about Charlene and the grits competition. You know, that police officer asked about my purse," Meredith said. "It would have been easy for a thief to grab it and run. But he didn't take it. He went for your wallet. That proves he was targeting you."

"He didn't say anything."

"No, he didn't, but I wish he would have." Meredith sighed. "Please, Julia, until we know more, don't go out alone, okay? And please tell Beau about this."

"I will. He won't be happy about it. I hate thinking that Prescott was watching me."

"I do too."

"But if he's after me, why just steal my wallet? He could have seriously hurt me if he'd wanted to. I don't understand."

"You said your driver's license was with your phone. But was there anything else in your wallet that had your address on it?"

Julia thought for a moment. "I don't think so. But I had agency cards in there with this address."

Meredith stared at her for a moment. "That worries me."

"Well, it doesn't make me feel good either, but if I think anyone's trying to follow me, I'll drive straight to the police station and get help."

"Beau may want to go everywhere with you for a while."

"He might, but I won't let him. Let's not worry until we're sure there's something to worry about." She smiled. "Now, let's get busy on our grits case." Julia laughed. "There's a sentence I never thought I'd say." She was still concerned about Prescott, but she needed to move on. If she kept thinking about him, she would start to unravel. She needed to focus on something else.

Meredith grinned. "It is strange, isn't it? I'm glad everyone recovered. A friend of mine called to let me know Ernie Prothro has been released from the hospital."

"Well, that's good news. So what's our next step?"

"I think we need to talk to the contestants. See if we can find out how that jar of ghost peppers ended up on the table."

Carmen came into the conference room, an odd look on her face. "That was Maggie Lu. Ernie Prothro followed through with his threat of a lawsuit. There's a story about it in the paper this morning. He's asking the police to charge Charlene and Maribelle with reckless endangerment. Can he really do that?"

"Reckless endangerment means conduct that involves disregard for the safety of others," Julia said. "Something that causes substantial risk of serious physical injury to another person. I doubt that eating hot pepper qualifies. If anyone could get sued, it might be the sponsors of the contest. Not Charlene and Maribelle. I can't believe the police will take this seriously. And no ethical attorney would take on a case like this."

Carmen shrugged. "Well, it seems someone has. Maggie Lu is very upset."

"We need to talk to those other competitors as soon as possible," Meredith said. "Before some ambulance chaser gets to them ahead of us and gums up the works."

"I agree," Julia said. Although she didn't like to hear attorneys called *ambulance chasers,* she was aware that unscrupulous people in the law profession jumped on cases that had no merit if they thought they could get someone to settle rather than go to court. Or if they thought it would get their names out to the public. That had to be the reason Prothro's attorney took this case. Reckless endangerment was a misdemeanor. Charlene wasn't rich, so it couldn't be that he was after her money.

"Well, let's decide who we need to talk to," Meredith said. "I hope they'll all cooperate."

"If they want to keep themselves above suspicion, they will," Julia said.

Carmen went back to her desk, and Meredith and Julia began making a list of the people they needed to contact.

"So what are you cookin' tonight?" Bessie asked.

Portia smiled. "Is your homework done, girl?"

"I'll do it in a minute," Bessie said, impatience in her voice. "I jes wanna know what we're havin' for supper. I might wants to add it to your recipe book."

"Bless your heart, Bessie. Are you still at that?"

"Yes'm. I have almost twelve of your recipes now. So what are we having for supper?"

Portia laughed. Her daughter was nothing if not persistent. Of course, that was a good thing. She would need to be stubborn to make it in the world. Some enslaved people had been set free, but it didn't seem to make much difference in many places. Freed Blacks had a hard time finding paid work or lodging in the South, even after the Emancipation Proclamation was signed.

"I'm fixin' gumbo, corn bread, and pecan pie," Portia said. "Your favorite."

"Oh, Mama, I love pecan pie more than...more than... Well, almost more than your grits."

Portia bit back another laugh. This child was something to behold. She thought praisin' her mama would get her anything she wanted. Most of the time that was probably true. But not when it came to schoolin'. It was the one thing that could change her life for the better. That and her belief in the

Almighty. Bessie would need His help once she left home and went out into the world.

"You go do your homework, and you do it good. Then after supper, we'll sit down and I'll tell you how I make gumbo and pecan pie. I's already given you the recipe for corn bread."

"All right," Bessie said with a sigh. "I won't be long. Tonight is writin' assignments. I like that. But I hate arithmetic. Addin' this and subtractin' that. Goodness' sakes."

"You need arithmetic for cookin', Bessie," Portia said. "If you don't know how much to put into your pot, it will come out wrong."

"But why do I need to know what will happen if I takes some away?" a frustrated Bessie asked. "Heavens to Betsy, it don't make much sense."

Portia stopped what she was doing and turned around to face her daughter. "We don't use the name of somethin' that belongs to the Lord and make it cheap," she said. "Don't you go sayin' heaven unless you plannin' on goin' there, understand?"

Bessie's eyes grew large. "I'm sorry, Mama. Some of the girls at school say it."

"Well, they mamas need to put a stop to it." She picked up her large wooden spoon and shook it at her daughter. "It's not gonna happen in my house."

"Sorry, Mama," she said again.

Bessie looked so hurt, Portia almost said something to soothe her, but she talked herself out of it. Young'uns needed to know how to act. She wouldn't have no child of hers take holy words in vain.

"You say you don't need to know 'bout takin' away things?" Portia asked.

A chastised Bessie just nodded.

"What if Miss Maisie takes sick? I want to fix her some gumbo. But my regular recipe is too big for her. What can I do?"

Bessie was quiet as she stared at her. Finally, she said, "You'd hafta make a smaller amount 'cause she couldn't eat all that and it wouldn't keep too long."

"That's right. So how do I figger out the right amount to take her?"

It was obvious to Portia that Bessie understood what she was saying.

"You'd have to subtract some of the fixin's."

Portia nodded. "And what if yo daddy needed to fix a hole in the fence so Lulu can't get out? We need her for the milk she gives us. Should he chop enough wood to put up a whole new side of that fence?"

"No, Mama. That would be silly. He just needs enough for the hole." Bessie sighed. "All right. I understand. We gotta learn how to subtract too." She shook her head. "This learnin' stuff is hard."

"Oh, Bessie," Portia said with a sigh. "You don't know hard. Not like yo daddy and me do. I jes hope that someday you'll have everythin' I keep prayin' for you." She couldn't stop the tears that slipped down her face. She picked up the corners of her apron and wiped her face.

"Mama, why you cryin'?" Bessie asked.

"Never mind," Portia said. "Now you go do your home-work 'fore I find another use for this spoon."

"Yes'm. I'm goin' now."

Portia smiled as Bessie sat down at the table and opened the tattered book given to her by Mother Mathilda. All she could get for the Black children were books that had been thrown away by white children. But still, Portia felt blessed. They were free, Cletus had work, and they had food. Not many Black people in the country had what her family had. She whispered a prayer of thanks as she stirred her pot of gumbo. In her heart she also prayed for the day when all people would be treated equally, as God intended.

Chapter Seven

JULIA CALLED THE POLICE DEPARTMENT and told a rather disinterested officer named Frett about Grady Prescott being in the area and that she believed he was the one who stole her wallet. When she explained that their assistant had drawn a picture of Prescott, he was quiet. "I assume you want this sketch?" she asked.

"So you had your assistant draw a picture of Prescott? Do you have any reason to believe he might try to steal something from you?"

"No. You don't understand. The wallet was stolen first. I didn't realize it was Prescott until later, when my friend described the thief to our assistant."

"All right, ma'am. You can bring a copy of the sketch to us. We'll check out this Prescott person."

"There's something else you need to know," Julia said. She explained that she was the prosecutor assigned to Prescott's trial and that he was sentenced to life in prison. The officer seemed a little more interested in that information but told her something she already knew. Unless Prescott made a direct threat to her or actually caused her bodily harm, there was nothing they could do. However, they would try to find him and question him in connection with the robbery.

When Julia hung up, she wasn't feeling encouraged by the officer's lack of concern. She found the theft more than coincidence, but there wasn't much she could do about it.

Her next call was to Mr. Andre's. She talked to the manager, who told her that although they had surveillance cameras, the man who tried to use the card wore a hat. His face wasn't visible. The clerk who'd served him had been questioned by the police, but she wasn't able to describe him beyond saying that he was a white man in a hat. It had been a very busy day at Mr. Andre's. Julia mentioned the scar, but the manager said the clerk didn't mention anything like that.

The information confused Julia. She didn't remember the man wearing a hat when he bumped into her.

She sighed with frustration. Prescott was probably going to get away with stealing her wallet.

She went into Meredith's office and sat down in one of her two olive-green designer chairs. Meredith's fireplace was almost identical to Julia's. This had once been a music room. An antique trumpet, a nod to the room's original use, sat on the mantel. The room had large windows that looked out on Forsythe Park. Julia loved the view. It soothed her.

"Mere, when Prescott bumped into me, was he wearing a hat?"

"A hat? No. Why?"

"I just got off the phone with the manager of Mr. Andre's. Their surveillance camera shows a man in a hat. He kept his head down so his face wasn't seen. The clerk who waited on him could only recall that he was a man in a hat."

"What about the scar?" Meredith asked.

Julia shook her head. "The clerk doesn't remember seeing one."

Meredith frowned. "I don't understand. Unless…"

"Unless what?"

"Maybe Prescott threw your wallet away. Perhaps the guy who tried to use your card found it. Or maybe Prescott put a hat on."

Julia sighed. "But what did Prescott want? Was he just trying to get close to me? Let me know he was out of prison?"

"Maybe he wanted your address."

"There are easier ways to get that information," Julia said. "I think our first impulse is the right one. Prescott wants me to know he's here. And that he can get to me if he wants to." Julia shook her head. "I should have recognized him immediately. Why didn't I?"

"Because you weren't thinking about him. You thought he was in prison. Your thoughts just didn't go that way."

"That's true. I guess I'd put him out of my mind." She smiled. "I really try not to think about past cases. It can drive you nuts. But if he really was innocent, I want to know about it. Frankly, I'd like to talk to him. Maybe he really was wrongly convicted."

Meredith sat back in her chair, a frown on her face. "Then he should have called and asked to speak to you, Julia. Not stolen your wallet."

"Yeah. I see your point." She clasped her hands. "Let's get back to the grits contest. We need to figure out what happened. Maggie Lu and Charlene are depending on us."

"You're right."

"Why don't we have lunch at Savannah Sally's? I know Sally Becker a little. She was involved in a mentoring group for disadvantaged kids when I worked for the juvenile court. She was different.

Kind of flighty, but I think she has a good heart. I believe she'll talk to us." Julia smiled. "Besides, she's got a crush on Beau."

Meredith laughed. "I don't think you need to worry about Beau. We could call her on the phone, Julia. Ask her about the competition. Surely you don't think we should eat at the restaurant of every finalist in the grits contest."

"I don't know. I'd rather talk to people face-to-face when I'm asking them important questions. You can see a lot more by observing them in person."

"Okay," Meredith said with a sigh.

"Let's take it restaurant by restaurant. I want to find a way to repair Charlene's reputation. If it makes you feel any better, Beau and I enjoy Sally's."

"Okay. We go to Savannah Sally's for lunch. But are you sure we'll be able to speak to her?"

Julia thought for a moment. "I'll call her and let her know we plan to come there for lunch today and ask her for a good time to talk."

"Are you going to tell her we're working for Charlene?"

Julia shrugged. "I think so. She seems like a decent person." She smiled. "Except for her habit of flirting with married men. In my opinion, innocent people should be happy to talk to us. The guilty ones…not so much."

"You're right."

Julia got up. "I'll call you and let you know what I find out."

"Sounds good," Meredith said.

Julia went to her office, her mind turning and twisting, full of pieces of a puzzle that didn't make sense. It would take effort to put Grady Prescott out of her mind for a while.

She looked up the number for Savannah Sally's and asked for Sally when someone answered. After a small delay, a high-pitched voice with a slow Southern drawl said, "Why, hello, Julia. So nice to hear from you. You and Beau have been scarce as hen's teeth lately."

"Sorry, Sally. It's certainly no reflection on your great food. Just really busy."

"Well, what in the world can I do for you, sugah?"

Julia explained about the lawsuit and assured Sally that Charlene and Maribelle had nothing to do with what happened at the competition.

"Why, for goodness' sake," Sally said. "I nevah thought they did. Somethin's afoot for sure, but I think that awful Laurel Hurst is involved somehow. You just can't believe anything that woman says. She's slicker than snot on a doorknob. I wouldn't trust her as far as I could throw her."

"Do you have any proof that Laurel was involved?"

There was a pause. "No, sugah. Not really. But I think she'd do anything to win that grits contest. Frankly, her grits are so heavy with cheese, you can't taste anything else. Nasty stuff." She sighed. "Strange things occurred during the preliminary rounds of the contest. One cook's cooler with all his ingredients disappeared. He certainly was upset. The police found it later with some kids who thought it would be funny to take it. He was allowed to enter the next round since it wasn't his fault he couldn't prepare his dish when he was assigned. Unfortunately, he was eliminated in that round. Then a couple of people complained because their entry applications didn't arrive in time. There was nothing that could be done. They waited until the last moment to mail them in. They could have delivered them by hand or even sent them priority mail. Everyone else got their applications and entry fees in on time. Goodness gracious, Laurel Hurst went on and on about it. Like I had anything to do with that." Another big sigh.

Julia needed to steer Sally back to the reason she was calling. "So what time would work for Meredith and me to come by?" she asked. "We don't want to bother you during your busy times."

"Why, hon, y'all can come by any time. What works for you?"

Julia glanced at the clock. "How about one?"

"Sure enough. Are you bringin' that handsome husband of yours?"

"Not this time, Sally," Julia said. "But we'll plan to get down there for supper before long."

"Just see that you do," Sally said lightly. "That man is a sight for sore eyes."

Julia chuckled. "Thanks, Sally. We'll see you at one."

After she hung up Julia contemplated telling Beau what Sally had said. But if she did he probably wouldn't want to eat at her restaurant anymore. He was a man and liked compliments, but Sally was more than a little overdone. She'd embarrassed him more than once. Julia sighed as she contemplated the investigation in front of them. All she could do was pray they could find out what really happened before Charlene's restaurant was hit hard by the accusations bandied about by Ernie Prothro. At some point they'd need to talk to him. That was a conversation she wasn't looking forward to.

Chapter Eight

WHEN JULIA AND MEREDITH ARRIVED at the restaurant, it was busy. Several people were waiting for a table. Before they approached the hostess, Sally saw them and hurried over.

"These ladies have a reservation," she told the hostess. She picked up menus and motioned for Julia and Meredith to follow her. She led them to a nice table away from the main part of the dining room, probably because it would be easier to talk privately.

Julia and Meredith sat down as Sally put their menus on the table. "Now you ladies order anything you want. It's on me."

"Oh no, Sally," Julia said. "We didn't expect you to treat us."

She waved her hand as if shooing Julia's comment away. "I won't take no for an answer." She smiled at Meredith and waited, obviously expecting an introduction.

"Sally, this is Meredith Bellefontaine, owner of Magnolia Investigations."

"Well, how do you do, Meredith?" Sally asked with a grin. "I'm so happy to meet you. Now you ladies enjoy your lunch. I'll sit down with you when you're done. How does that sound?"

Julia thought about saying something again about Sally buying their meals, but she knew it was a lost cause. She just nodded and thanked her.

When Sally walked away, Meredith said, "Wow. She's something else."

Julia agreed. "She is a handful. But I can't see her as the kind of person who would cheat to win a grits competition. She has a successful restaurant, and frankly, grits aren't her signature dish."

Meredith scanned the menu. "Seems like her most emphasized specialty is the fried chicken and catfish."

"Yes, but her turkey sandwich is… Well, you'll love it."

"I see it comes with homemade potato salad and deviled eggs."

Julia smiled. "Yes, and it's all delicious. Order the sandwich and sides. Trust me."

Meredith closed her menu. "Okay. So what are you getting?"

"I usually get the fried chicken, but I've been so busy talking you into this sandwich, now I want one."

Meredith laughed. "My goodness. We're twins."

"Except I'm not ordering Diet Dr Pepper today. I think I'll go with raspberry iced tea."

"I'm shocked," Meredith said with a grin. "Who are you and what did you do with my friend?"

"Ha ha. Very funny."

The waitress came to their table and took their order. As they waited, Julia looked around the restaurant. It really was a pleasant place. Sally had used soft ivory tones with gold accents to create a classy but calming atmosphere. Brick walls painted a soft white with gold sconces and portraits of famous Southern aristocracy worked together to create an elegant but not overdone Southern-style eating establishment. Julia also liked that the acoustics kept the noise down to a level that made it possible to have a conversation. She detested restaurants that drummed loud music into the ears of its patrons or were designed in a way that voices were amplified. It was like being stuck in the middle of a heated argument that you couldn't understand. Awful. But Savannah Sally's was a place you could comfortably visit with friends.

Not long after placing their order, the waitress came back with their food.

"My goodness gracious," Meredith exclaimed when she saw her sandwich. "It's huge."

Julia grinned. "You'll probably want to take half of it home and eat it later. Beau usually does."

Meredith turned over the top slice of sourdough bread. "Mayo and lettuce. Just how I like it." She added a generous amount of salt and pepper and then put the bread back on top.

There were pickles, onions, and a tomato slice on the side as optional toppings.

Meredith ignored those as Julia knew she would. Meredith loved turkey sandwiches with only mayo and lettuce. Anything else was seen as a betrayal to the purity of the sandwich. Julia added the tomato and pickles to hers.

After they said grace Meredith picked up her sandwich and took a bite. Her eyes widened as she swallowed.

"Oh, Julia. This might be the best turkey sandwich I've ever tasted. It reminds me of Thanksgiving. My mother would roast a huge turkey. For days after Thanksgiving we ate turkey sandwiches with chips and finished it off with pumpkin pie." She smiled. "Thank you for suggesting this. I wonder why I haven't been here before."

Julia laughed. "I assume it's because Savannah is overflowing with restaurants. We can't visit every one."

Meredith nodded her agreement. Both she and Julia ate half of their sandwiches and had to ask for carryout boxes.

"The potato salad and deviled eggs were delicious too. There are none left," Julia said as she put the rest of her sandwich in the box. She'd just closed it when Sally swooped into the room. *Swoop* was the right word. Sally Becker was a force to be reckoned with. A human dynamo.

Other people in the restaurant stopped what they were doing or saying and watched her as she glided toward Julia and Meredith's table.

Sally, who was wearing a white dress with a lace bodice and a lace overlay, settled into the chair next to Julia. Her blond hair was swept up into a messy bun that Julia suspected was actually carefully constructed. Sally fastened her blue eyes on Julia. "So how were those sandwiches?"

"The best I've ever tasted," Meredith said with a smile.

Sally's eyes locked on Julia's. Obviously she was waiting for her response.

"Absolutely delicious," Julia said truthfully. She couldn't tell Sally that her sandwich was the best she'd ever had. Sandwiches made from her grandma Gertrude's turkey would always hold the top spot in her heart.

"Now, what did you ladies want to know about Friday night?" she asked.

Julia lowered her voice, hoping Sally would get the idea. People were starting to talk again, but their muted conversations made Julia wonder if they were listening. She and Meredith needed to investigate without alerting the entire clientele of Savannah Sally's what they were up to.

"We were wondering if you noticed anything unusual the night of the competition," Julia said in hushed tones.

Sally made a sound that sounded like *pfft.* "I noticed that Ernie Prothro almost passed out when he tasted my grits. I actually had to grab him before he hit the ground." She sighed as she stroked her skirt. "And then Beverly upchucked, you know." She patted her hair. "It was quite a mess. I do declare, I won't be eatin' grits for quite a while." She gave a little ladylike shiver.

"What about the jar that held the ground peppers?" Meredith asked. "Did you see who brought it to the table?"

Sally paused for a moment before saying, "I did not, but Cyrus Sharrah told me it was Jerome. Cyrus said that a little while before the event started Jerome put it on the table and said that the judges wanted the dishes to have color. And that one of them—I think it was Ernie Prothro—would mark down our entries if we didn't finish it with a splash of paprika. Had something to do with how the finished dishes looked on TV. Since it doesn't add much flavor, I decided to use it. I didn't want to lose the contest over something so trivial."

Julia noticed that Sally's Southern accent was somewhat muted. It was clear much of her affected manner was for the benefit of her customers.

Sally's eyes grew wide, and she sat up straight. "Well, shut my mouth. I should have known it. Jerome works for Laurel Hurst. She must be behind this. It had to be her. She set this contest up so she'd win and show the rest of us up. Then she—" Sally stared at Julia. "That just doesn't make sense though, does it? Why would she ruin her own grits?"

"And why not use something that would just make the other contestants' grits taste bad?" Meredith asked. "Really, hot pepper is going to cause an immediate and disastrous reaction."

"You're right," Sally said. "Well, here I was gettin' ready to accuse Laurel. But now I see that dog don't hunt." She shook her head. "Doesn't seem like I've helped you ladies much, and I surely am sorry."

Julia had to bite back a smile. The Southern lady returned as she prepared to walk among her patrons.

"You told us something we didn't know before," Julia said. "The truth always gets us closer to a solution."

"Well, I hope you find the varmint behind this. Goodness gracious, even a blind hog finds an acorn now and then." With that and a blinding smile Sally rose from the table and began circulating from table to table, beguiling her customers with her Southern charm.

"Well, if Sally is telling the truth, we know who put the jar on the table," Julia said quietly to Meredith.

"But that doesn't prove Laurel Hurst is behind it," Meredith said. "They would be stupid to put that container on the table in plain sight." She frowned. "By the way, did Sally just call us hogs?"

Julia laughed. "I don't think she meant it that way. You know, I still can't see why anyone would put ghost pepper in the paprika container. No one wins the contest that way. Even if a chef declined to use it, the entire contest would be canceled. No one would come out the victor."

"That's been bothering me as well." Meredith leaned closer to Julia. "It's almost like someone wasn't actually targeting a person. It's as if they were trying to ruin the contest itself. But why?"

Chapter Nine

JULIA AND MEREDITH WENT BACK to the office. They'd no sooner parked and walked in the back door when Carmen hurried up to them.

"You've got a visitor," she said, her eyes wide. "It's that Ernie Prothro. You know, the guy from the newspaper?"

"Goodness, what's he doing here?" Meredith asked.

"Well, it will save us from trying to get an appointment with him," Julia said. "Let's meet with him in your office."

Meredith nodded. "I'll call you when we're ready for him."

Julia went into her own office and grabbed her notebook and a pen. This should be interesting. Ernie was a legend in his own mind. He'd gotten the position at the *Savannah Tribune* when the former food editor, Boog Simpson, was asked to retire early. Frankly, Julia was grateful. Boog's name conjured up pictures in her mind she didn't want.

Once they were ready, Meredith called Carmen and asked her to escort Prothro to her office.

Moments later, Ernie walked through the door. He certainly looked like a food editor, tall and portly. His bald head reflected the light from the overhead fixture.

"Thank you for seeing me," he said. "I understand you are representing the Downhome Diner in the matter of the lawsuit I intended to file?"

"Well, no," Meredith said. "We're not attorneys. We're investigators. Julia and I are simply trying to find out what happened. We know Charlene Jackson had nothing to do with the unfortunate incident at the grits competition. We intend to uncover the truth."

Ernie gestured toward the chair in front of Meredith's desk. "May I sit?"

"Of course," Meredith said.

Ernie sighed and lowered himself into the chair. "I am here to offer my mea culpa. There is no lawsuit. After conferring with my attorneys this morning, I've dropped all action against your clients. I regret my abrupt reaction. I was angry and was attempting to seek retribution for my…near poisoning." He glared at them. "I assume you're aware that people have died from ingesting too many hot peppers."

Meredith cleared her throat. "Well, from eating a lot of the actual peppers, yes. But I don't think taking a bite of powdered ghost peppers has ever killed anyone."

Ernie's face flushed red. "Ghost pepper? I had no idea. Extremely dangerous no matter what form they take. The pain was horrible. It took two days for me to be able to taste food again."

Julia prepared herself for one of his rather famous rages. He was known for a hot temper. But to his credit he took a deep breath and his cheeks slowly returned to a normal color.

"But of course you're right," he said. "The actual pepper is much more lethal. It could have been worse."

Trying to ignore his habit of holding his nose high as if smelling something unpleasant, Julia said, "I'm curious. May I ask why you decided not to pursue your suit?"

"Well, my lawyers told me my chances were slim and that even if someone were found guilty, the recompense wouldn't be much more than my hospital bill. I'd thought there might be reimbursement for pain and suffering, but I realize now that I was being petty. I'm terribly sorry I ever brought it up." He gave them a smile that looked all too forced. He took another deep breath. "I wonder if you would extend my apologies to Charlene and her chef."

"Perhaps you should talk to them yourself," Julia said.

Ernie stood up from his chair. "You may be correct, but right now I'm somewhat embarrassed by my actions. Perhaps at a later date I may be able to do as you suggest."

"What about that story in the *Tribune*?" Meredith asked. "Will you state publicly that you're not following through on your threat?"

"Already done. I've been assured they'll print a correction." He gave the women a little bow and left the office.

Julia waited until she heard the front door close before saying, "Well, that was interesting." She gazed at Meredith. "What do you think? I felt like he was..."

"Being forced to drop the lawsuit?"

"Exactly." Julia mused for a moment. "I'll bet his attorneys really did talk him out of it. Like he said, there wasn't much of a case. And it would have cost him more to pay his lawyers than he could have gotten even if he was able to win a judgment...which I doubt. I certainly wouldn't have taken his case if he'd come to me when I was practicing. In fact, Charlene could have filed a countersuit. And probably won."

"I think you're right," Meredith said slowly. "I also sensed a kind of panic in him. I have a feeling someone pointed out that the case was weak and he could end up looking like a bully. Newspapers want their high-profile personalities to be likable."

Julia nodded. "Well, at least this is good news. Something we can tell Charlene that should lift some of the burden she's been under."

"Yes. She'll probably tell us to drop the case."

Julia raised an eyebrow. "We're not charging her anything…"

"So if we want to keep investigating…"

"We can," Julia said, laughing. "I really want to know what happened. *Someone* replaced the paprika for a reason, and right now, I have no earthly idea why. We need to find out."

"I agree."

Julia heard the door open again. "Wow, this is Grand Central Station today," she said.

They waited, and then Charlene came into the office. "I'm sorry," she said. "I realize I should wait for you to contact me, and I know it's early, but…"

"It's okay," Julia said with a smile. "We were just getting ready to call you. Ernie Prothro dropped the lawsuit."

Charlene looked unsteady on her feet, and Julia got up and took her by the arm, lowering her into the chair Ernie had just vacated.

"I can hardly believe it," she said. "What did you do?"

Meredith smiled. "Nothing. He just walked in here and told us he couldn't go forward. Was very apologetic."

Charlene looked surprised. "Apologetic? Ernie Prothro? That's against his nature."

"We were thinking the same thing," Julia said. "We both felt like he was here out of obligation. Not because he wanted to drop his so-called case."

"I wish we knew who put that jar on the table," Charlene said.

"But we do know," Julia said. "We talked to Sally Becker earlier today. She said Cyrus Sharrah told her that Jerome Matheson actually placed it there."

Charlene's eyes widened. "Why?"

"That's what we don't know. And I guess we'll never find out… I mean now that we don't work for you anymore."

Charlene looked confused for a moment. Then she laughed. "Who said you aren't still working for me?"

Julia grinned. "Then we'll keep digging. And the price is the same."

"I really can't let you do that," Charlene said.

"Don't be silly," Meredith said. "You and your mom are family. Besides, your diner is our favorite place to discuss our cases, so we have a vested interest in your business."

"Well, if you come in, at least I'll have two customers," Charlene said glumly.

"What are you saying?" Julia asked. "Your customers love you. I can't believe you'll lose any business out of this."

"We have some very loyal customers," Charlene agreed, "but they don't make up all of our traffic. As you know, Savannah gets a lot of tourists. When they read something in the paper about us…"

"It worries them." Julia shook her head. "This contest was supposed to bring in new business, not make you lose it."

"Maybe if you find out what really happened, I can get my reputation back." Charlene sighed. "Of course, getting the word out might be tough. My guess is the story about Ernie dropping his lawsuit will be hidden on page forty in the *Tribune*, next to the obituaries." She held her hand up as if writing something. "Downhome Diner passed away in October from a lack of business and a ruined reputation. In lieu of flowers, please send money so its staff can be paid."

"Let's not get ahead of ourselves," Meredith scolded. "A little faith will help you hang in there while we figure out who was behind this…and what they hoped to achieve by doing something so foolish."

Charlene stood and walked to the door. "Thank you," she said. "You're such good friends."

"We're happy to do whatever we can to help," Meredith said.

After Charlene left, Meredith turned to Julia. "Why would Jerome Matheson try to ruin the grits contest? I understand Laurel's grits are excellent. She had a good chance of winning."

"I don't know." Julia thought for a moment. "We need to talk to Maribelle. I want to know what she remembers about that jar of 'paprika.'"

"If she knew anything more, wouldn't she have said something Friday night?" Meredith asked. "Or have talked to Charlene?"

"Probably, but things were moving pretty fast. Maybe she never got the chance. Or she might have forgotten something important." Julia straightened up in her chair and picked up the phone. "I'd like to know exactly what Jerome said when he put the pepper on the table. I know what Sally said, but I think we need to be sure, don't you?"

Meredith sighed. "If you tell me we have to go to the diner for supper, I don't know what I'm going to do. My waistline is going to be a thing of the past."

Julia shrugged. "Then I guess I can just roll you around because we are going to the diner for supper."

As Julia dialed the number of the diner, she heard Meredith groan.

Chapter Ten

"Mama, you got to slow down," Bessie said. "I'm havin' a hard time writin' everything down."

"I told you, child, that it's all in my head. You're makin' me use these measurin' things from Mother Mathilda. It makes me nervous."

"But Mama, this will help other people understand what's in your head." Bessie sighed. "Don't you want these recipes passed down through years and years? Jes think. A hundred years from now, some lady will be makin' your shrimp and grits. And your jambalaya and corn bread. Some children like me will be smackin' their lips about your pecan pie. And your sweet potato pie. And chicken 'n' dumplings. And Mama, you make the best fried chicken in the whole world."

Portia turned to look at her daughter. "Wait jes a minute. You sure is addin' things up fast. I can't measure all that food." Although she wasn't sure she could give Bessie what she wanted, the excitement on her daughter's face melted Portia's *heart. "You know this could take a while. When does Mother Mathilda want her measurin' doo-dads back?"*

"She said you could keep 'em, Mama. They's yours."

Portia sighed. "All right. It sure seems you're determined to do this, so I'll do the best I can. But you better be patient."

"I will be, Mama," Bessie said, her eyes shining.

Portia turned back to the stove. What in the world had gotten into this young one? She wasn't sure, but she knew Bessie was proud of her...and her cooking. She stared at the spoons and cups sitting on the counter. Then she sighed and picked up the one Bessie said measured a cup. Maybe she could do this after all. Was it true that a hundred years from now someone might actually be making her shrimp and grits? Wouldn't that be something?

Julia and Meredith waited around until after the diner closed so Maribelle could talk to them. Julia loved the old diner with its yellow walls and prints of Old Savannah that included a vintage map of Savannah from 1734, the National Bank Building at the turn of the twentieth century, and Fort Jackson on the banks of the Savannah River. However, her very favorite things were the red vinyl-covered stools that ran the length of the diner. Her grandfather had brought her here when she was a little girl, and she could remember spinning on her stool. Her grandfather would make her stop and tell her she needed to act like a "proper Southern lady," but the sparkle in his eyes made it clear he found her actions amusing. As she and Meredith ate, Julia watched another little girl spin on a stool just like she had. It made her glad to see that children still appreciated the diner.

After finishing their meals, they waited for Maribelle to join them. When she came out of the back room, she had on a dark blue dress with little white flowers. She always wore dresses. Julia had never seen her in pants. She and her husband, Chester, belonged to a local United Pentecostal Church where the women were encouraged to wear dresses, but she was never judgmental toward other women who wore slacks or jeans. Maribelle was a friendly, loving person, but also very determined if she thought she was right.

"Sorry for takin' so long," she said as she took a seat. She pulled a white handkerchief from her purse and wiped the beads of sweat from her dark forehead. "Charlene said you wanted to talk about the contest?"

Just then, Charlene walked up to the table. "Do you mind if I join you?" she asked. "I don't want to butt in."

Julia smiled at her. "The more the merrier."

"Let's get everyone something to drink." Charlene turned around and motioned to one of the waitresses. "Tara, would you mind getting us some raspberry tea?"

The diner's raspberry tea was incredible. Julia had tasted it in other restaurants, but the diner's was the best. She quickly downed the rest of her Diet Dr Pepper in anticipation.

As Tara scurried off to get the tea, Julia smiled at Maribelle. "You told us that you didn't see who put the pepper jar on the table the night of the contest. But someone informed us it was Jerome Matheson from Mama Louise's Kitchen. I wondered if knowing that might jog your memory."

Maribelle scrunched up her face, obviously trying to think. "He did come over to one of the tables, I remember that now." She snapped her fingers, and her expression changed. "I do recall something. I'd gone back to my cooler to get out our finishing spice. When I came back I saw the jar of paprika and noticed Jerome walkin' away. I never put two and two together. It could have been him." She shook her head. "But I also saw Cyrus walking away from the table. I did say somethin' about it to that Martin guy from the Seaside Grill, but he just said it was there in case anyone needed it. Pretty strange, if you ask me. I'd never add another ingredient at the last minute. My grits were just the way I wanted them. There was no reason for that spice to be on the table."

"Supposedly, one of the reasons was so the dish would look better on TV," Meredith said. "Still, I would have assumed the contestants wouldn't be interested in adding something that's not in their original recipe."

"Well, I've seen my share of contests, and I've never seen anything like that," Charlene said. "But wanting to make the dishes look good on television makes some sense, I guess."

Julia nodded. "Seems like we're going to have to talk to Jerome."

"If you tell me we're going to Mama Louise's Kitchen…," Meredith said.

Julia laughed. "What about tomorrow afternoon? We can stop by for coffee and dessert."

Meredith sighed. "I suppose."

"I truly wish I could help you," Maribelle said. "I hate that this happened."

"Between what occurred at the contest and the robbery at the coin store, Friday was quite a night for the police," Charlene said.

"Robbery?" Julia asked. "What do you mean?"

"Haven't you heard? Hudson's Rare Coins was robbed Friday night at the same time the police were trying to find out what happened at the contest. Someone called the police and told them that one of the judges was dead, the others were seriously ill—and that it was an intentional poisoning."

"What?" Julia asked. "Where did you hear this?"

"From a customer this morning," Charlene said. "When you own a restaurant, you have access to more news than even the best reporters in town."

"That's why so many police officers showed up at the contest," Maribelle said. "They really thought someone was dead."

"Seems like they should have been at the coin shop instead of worryin' about us," Charlene added.

"How much was stolen?" Meredith asked.

Maribelle made a clucking sound. "I guess the thieves got away with over half a million dollars."

Julia's jaw dropped. "My goodness. I've heard of them but had no idea they had such a valuable inventory."

"They don't usually," Charlene said, "but they'd acquired a special coin. Something they were planning to sell to a man in Savannah who wanted to buy it. Although they tried to keep it quiet, I guess the news got out. While the police were messin' with us, the thieves made their move."

Julia and Meredith looked at each other. Finally, the grits fiasco was beginning to make some sense.

Chapter Eleven

JULIA AWAKENED TO A RAINY Tuesday morning. As she swung her legs over the side of the bed, she realized Beau wasn't there. She could hear the sound of dishes clattering in the other room. She slid on her slippers and grabbed her robe. When she got to the kitchen she found Beau standing over the stove.

"What are you up to?" she asked.

He turned around and smiled at her. "Good morning. Woke up a little early and decided I wanted to make you breakfast."

Beau didn't cook often, but when he did he was actually pretty good at it. He'd changed his eating habits ever since his triple bypass surgery. Although he still ate many of the foods he liked, it was with moderation. Julia tried to keep an eye on him by finding dishes that were heart-healthy but also delicious.

"What are we having?" she asked.

"Buttermilk pumpkin waffles," he said. "With a side of turkey sausage."

Julia gave her husband a hug. "What a blessing. It's been a tough week, and it's only Tuesday."

Beau hugged her back before letting her go. "You run out of here some mornings without breakfast and then grab something unhealthy to eat on the way to work. I wanted to give you a better option than the doughnuts you eat almost every day."

"I do not eat doughnuts every day," she said, laughing. "But I agree that I certainly could eat healthier."

The aroma of the waffles and the sizzling sausage made her stomach rumble. "I love these waffles. I can still have coffee, can't I?"

Beau laughed. "Yes, you can have coffee."

Julia sat down on a stool next to the granite island in their kitchen while Beau poured her a cup.

"Trying to find out what happened at the grits contest is like trying to put together a puzzle with some of the pieces missing." She stopped for a moment. "I take that back. It's more like someone stuck pieces from other puzzles into the box. I'm trying to put a picture together without knowing if I'm using the right pieces...or the wrong ones."

"What do you mean?" After handing Julia her coffee, Beau took a waffle out of the waffle iron and plopped a pat of butter on top. Then he added sugar-free syrup and placed a patty of turkey sausage on the plate.

Julia told him about the robbery Friday night. "Meredith and I wonder if the disaster at the grits contest was a diversion so the thieves would have more time to get away from the coin shop. One of Charlene's customers said that the police were told someone had been poisoned and died. It's the reason we had such a huge police presence."

Beau's thick gray eyebrows arched. "No kidding?" He put Julia's plate in front of her and gave her a napkin and a fork. Then he went back to the waffle iron to make himself one. "That sounds pretty compelling. I don't believe in coincidences. Sounds planned to me."

"Yeah, me too." Julia took a bite of her waffle. It was delicious.

"What about this Prescott fellow?" Beau asked.

Julia swallowed and washed the pancake down with coffee before speaking. "Here's the problem. He couldn't possibly be involved in the robbery, because he was at the contest when the theft was happening." She shook her head. "The weird thing is, Meredith and I are his alibi."

"Very convenient."

"Yes, it is." The timing bothered Julia, but there was no way Prescott could be running into her and robbing the coin store at the same time.

Beau put his plate on the island and sat down next Julia. "I really am sorry about the picture and the note. We should have made copies of both of them."

Julia nodded. "You're right. I wasn't thinking. Of course, a copy of the letter…"

"Isn't the actual letter your father wrote. I know. But aren't the words the most important thing, honey?"

"You're right, of course," Julia said. "I'm being silly, I guess. Except for the cash, I haven't actually lost anything. I have the memory of that day with my father, and I have the words he wrote stored in my heart. No one can take that away from me."

Beau leaned over and kissed her on the cheek. "Exactly."

Julia was just finishing her breakfast when the phone rang. When she answered, she recognized the voice of the police officer she'd talked to about the theft of her wallet.

"Mrs. Foley? This is Officer Frett. I took the report about your wallet?"

"Yes, I remember you."

"I have some good news. The company that picks up trash on River Street found it. Seems someone tried to toss it into a dumpster but missed. It was on the ground, and one of the maintenance workers found it."

"Oh, that's wonderful," Julia exclaimed.

"I have no idea if all your credit cards are here, and the cash is gone...."

"Officer Frett, there's a pocket behind the place for the cards. Will you look to see if there's a letter and a picture?"

There was silence for a moment before he said, "Yes, ma'am. They're here."

Julia almost cried with relief. "Thank you. Thank you so much. Can I come by and get it? I mean unless you need to dust it for fingerprints?"

"I'm sorry, Mrs. Foley, but we don't do that for thefts this small. Besides, by now there will be so many prints, it would be impossible to distinguish one from another."

Julia sighed. She knew that would be his response, but she had to ask. "Okay. Officer Frett, have you arrested anyone for the theft at the coin shop the night of the grits contest?"

Another silence. "No, ma'am. Do you have information about the robbery? If you do, you need to tell me."

"No, I'm sorry. I don't have any idea who the thieves are, but don't you find it odd that the problems at the contest and the robbery happened simultaneously?"

"I don't follow you."

"I heard that someone called you, claiming people were poisoned and that a death had occurred. Isn't that true?"

"Yes," Officer Frett said slowly. "How do you know about that?"

"I have a friend who overheard something. She passed it along to me as a rumor. Neither of us was certain it was true."

She hoped he wasn't going to ask who had told her. She wanted to keep Maribelle and Charlene out of this. Especially since Maribelle's grits were the only ones that didn't receive a dose of ghost pepper.

"When the police arrived the night of the contest you would have thought people were dropping like flies rather than there being only two people who were sickened by the pepper," Julia continued. "I mean, did it slow your response to the coin robbery? Would you have gotten there faster if your focus hadn't been on the grits contest?"

"Well, yes. I guess so. So you think they're connected?"

"I do," Julia said. "Don't you?" She wanted to ask him for details about the coin shop robbery, but she didn't want to push her luck. She decided to wait. Maybe she and Meredith could visit the coin shop themselves. She was convinced the timing wasn't a coincidence.

Officer Frett cleared his throat. "I'll bring it up to my boss. See what he says. We do have crimes that happen close together, you know. It's really not that unusual."

"I'm sure that's true, but the situation at the grits contest... It just doesn't make any sense. No one gained anything out of what happened. I can't help but wonder if it was a diversion."

"Do you suspect anyone? This Prescott guy you told me about?"

"Well, if he was at the grits contest he could hardly be at the coin shop, could he?"

"I suppose not," Frett said with a sigh. "Well, no matter what, I'm glad your wallet was found. I asked the maintenance worker for his contact information so you could thank him, but he declined. Just said he was happy he could help you."

"I wish he'd left his name. I'm so grateful."

"I know you're looking into what happened at the grits contest," Frett said. "If you find anything that will help us, please let me know?"

"Absolutely," Julia said. "We'll contact you immediately."

"Thank you, Mrs. Foley. Have a good day."

When Julia hung up, Beau said, "What's going on?"

"Someone turned in my wallet. The letter and the picture are still inside."

"Why, that's wonderful," Beau said with a wide smile. "Why don't you look happier? I thought you'd be dancing a jig to get that news."

Julia raised one eyebrow. "I'm certain I will never *dance a jig* over anything, but I am really thrilled to get it back."

"Then why the sour expression?"

Julia sighed. "This isn't my sour expression. This is my thoughtful expression."

"Sorry," Beau said. "I get those mixed up sometimes. So why the *thoughtful* expression?"

Julia laughed. "You're ridiculous, you know that?"

"Yes, I'm aware. Now…"

"Well, maybe it really is a coincidence, but you know that Grady Prescott was convicted of armed robbery."

"And was exonerated."

"Yes. But think about it. Someone causes a tumult at the grits contest, a coin shop is robbed, and I run into Grady Prescott. All these things happened at about the same time."

"But if he's connected to any of this, why would he bump into you? Steal your wallet? If he wanted to get away with a crime, why would he let you know he was in town? If he hadn't bumped into you, his name would never have entered your head. I don't get it."

"I don't either, but I have this feeling that it's important. I can't prove it, but I'm sure now that Prescott knew exactly who I was."

"Give me a minute and I'll get dressed," Beau said.

"I don't understand...."

"Just call me your shadow. I'll be driving you to work and back for a while. I don't want you going anywhere alone until Prescott leaves the state or ends up in jail."

Julia started to protest, but he held his hand up.

"I don't want to hear it, Julia. This man may have gotten out of prison, but I don't like the way he did it. I think he knows his way around guns, and he may be blaming you for his incarceration. I insist on driving you."

She thought about arguing, but Beau's determined expression made it clear she wouldn't get anywhere. She gave him a kiss on the cheek then hurried to get dressed.

Before she left, she made sure her handgun was in her purse. She'd never had to use it and prayed she never would. If Prescott really was innocent, no harm done. But if he wasn't, she had to take precautions.

Chapter Twelve

AFTER THEY PICKED UP HER wallet at the police station, Beau drove Julia to work. She had called Meredith to let her know she'd be late but didn't tell her why. She wanted to surprise her.

As they drove to the station and then to the office, Julia found herself looking around, watching the cars next to them. If Prescott was innocent, and she'd helped send him to prison, could he be even more of a threat than she'd first thought?

She kept trying to figure out how all three events on Friday night could be connected, but in the end, she wasn't sure they were. Coincidences happened, but still she couldn't let go of a nagging feeling that there was something fishy going on.

When they reached the office, she gave Beau a kiss and promised to call him when she was ready to leave.

When she got inside she grabbed a cup of coffee and asked Carmen to step into Meredith's office. Meredith was on her laptop, but she looked up when Julia and Carmen came in.

"I have a surprise," Julia said with a smile. "And I knew you'd both want to know about it."

"What is it?" Meredith asked.

Julia opened her purse and took out her wallet. She held it up for both women to see.

Meredith stood up and clapped her hands together. "Oh, Julia, I'm so happy! See, I told you you'd get it back."

"That's awesome!" Carmen said. "I've been praying."

"Thank you," Julia said.

"What about the picture and the letter?" Meredith asked.

Julia pulled them out of the pocket in the wallet. Tears burned her eyes. She was so grateful for their return.

"Now, put them somewhere else," Carmen said, wagging her finger at Julia.

"Trust me, I will." She sighed. "I kept them here so they would be close to me. But I'm not taking any more chances. I'll keep them at home where they'll be safe."

"I think you should have some copies made too," Meredith said. "It couldn't hurt."

"You're right." Julia put her wallet back in her purse. "Let me put this in my office. I have something else I'd like to talk about."

"We'll have to do it quickly. Adelaide Bridges, from *Southern Eats* magazine, is stopping by on her way to work."

"Isn't she the judge who sampled Maribelle's grits?" Julia asked. "The only one who didn't get sick?"

Meredith nodded. "Just want to make sure we cover all our bases. I told her we were investigating the incident, and she agreed to come by and talk to us."

"She's probably so grateful she didn't get sick, she'll do anything to help us."

Meredith laughed. "And I wouldn't blame her."

"I agree," Julia said. "I want to put my purse up. Be right back."

She hurried to her office and put her purse in the lower drawer of her desk. Then she went back to Meredith's office. Carmen had returned to her own desk.

"What did you want to talk about?" Meredith asked.

"When I talked to the police officer who called about my purse..." She heard the front door open. A woman asked for Meredith. It had to be Adelaide.

"We can talk about it after Adelaide leaves," she said quietly.

Meredith nodded.

Carmen brought Adelaide back to Meredith's office. Meredith stood and extended her hand. "I'm so grateful you took time out of your busy schedule to talk to us."

Adelaide shook hands with Meredith, and then turned to Julia.

"This is my partner, Julia Foley," Meredith said.

"Nice to meet you," Adelaide said, shaking her hand as well.

"You too. Please, have a seat," Julia said, motioning to the chair next to her.

"Thank you."

Adelaide had worked for *Southern Eats* magazine for many years. Her dark hair was swept up and held in place by a jeweled comb. Her dress was a soft pastel number that hugged her body and oozed elegance. The only thing about Adelaide that seemed a little *off* was her face. It looked rather frozen. As if she had a hard time moving her muscles. Julia had seen this before and suspected she'd recently had Botox injections.

"So have you discovered who poisoned the other judges?" Adelaide asked when she sat down. Even her Southern accent was perfect. Just slight. It added to her overall image.

"No, not yet," Meredith said. "We wanted to talk to you about that night. See if you noticed anything that might help us."

Adelaide frowned. "Well, I thought the idea of putting paprika on one of the tables where the contestants were set up was odd. I've never seen anything like that done in a food contest before."

"Adelaide, do you know whose idea it was to do that?" Julia asked.

"We heard that Ernie Prothro likes paprika on his grits, and believed the winning entry should have color." She paused for a moment. "Someone also mentioned that the finished dishes would look better on TV with a dusting of paprika. I can't remember who said it though."

"And is that true?" Meredith asked.

"It's possible." Adelaide frowned again. "I assume the contestants heard about it and decided to add paprika in an attempt to curry Ernie's favor. Still, it was unusual. Of course, the Downhome Diner brought their own seasoning, which was first rate, by the way."

"I probably shouldn't ask this," Julia said. "But do you think the diner might have won the contest?"

Adelaide smiled. "Their dish was wonderful. I feel confident they would have had a great chance if the contest hadn't been sabotaged."

"We were told that Jerome Matheson actually put the paprika on the table," Meredith said. "Can you confirm that?"

Adelaide shook her head. "I was talking to the reporter from Channel 4. The jar was already there by the time I got to the tables where the contestants were set up."

"Did you notice anything unusual that night?" Julia asked. "I realize it seems as if we're being a little pushy, but our friend's reputation is at stake."

"I saw that story in the *Tribune*," Adelaide said. "Very unfortunate. The Downhome Diner has wonderful food. I would hate to see what happened besmirch them in any way."

"The lawsuit was dropped," Meredith said, "but the accusations alone could cause damage to the diner."

"I understand." Adelaide took a deep breath and let it out slowly. To her credit, it was clear that she wanted to remember exactly what had been said. Finally, she said, "I'm sorry. There's just nothing I can tell you that would help you." She paused a moment. "I watched as some of the entrants used the paprika. I mean, there's nothing wrong with dusting a grits dish with paprika to give it color. But as I said, usually a chef won't make any last-minute changes that affect the flavor or presentation. I thought about saying something, but it wasn't my call. I was only there to judge. How the dishes were prepared and finished wasn't my business." She stood to her feet. "I'm afraid I'm not much help. Perhaps if I would have added some input at the time we would have avoided a…disaster. But again, it wasn't my job to tell anyone what to do with their food. I didn't want to be seen as giving advice when I would soon be judging their dishes. It could be seen as a conflict of interest. As if I were trying to help someone win the contest. I didn't want to compromise myself that way."

Meredith and Julia both stood up. "We understand. Thank you so much for your time," Meredith said.

"You're welcome. I hope the truth comes out. Please keep me in the loop."

"We will," Julia said.

Adelaide left the office. When she heard the front door close, Julia sat down again and sighed. "What do you think?" she asked Meredith, who eased back into her soft leather desk chair.

"Someone had to have seen something that night." She sighed. "We just need to keep digging until we uncover the truth."

Chapter Thirteen

November 1871

Bessie was working hard on the book that held her mama's recipes. Every afternoon when she got home from school, she quickly did her chores and homework. Then she sat down at the kitchen table and wrote down whatever her mama told her. She was happy with everything she had—corn bread, jambalaya, sweet potato pie, pecan pie, fried chicken, fried catfish, and potato soup. All great recipes, but she still didn't have her mama's shrimp and grits recipe. It was Bessie's favorite food in the whole world. Why did it seem as if Mama didn't want to share it?

"Can you give me your grits recipe now?" she asked her mother, who was standing over her woodstove stirring something.

Mama turned to look at her. "Hold your horses, Bessie Mae. You have lots of my recipes. Why are you so stirred up about my shrimp and grits?"

Bessie frowned. "I guess it's because I love them so much, Mama. Someday you'll be gone. I want to fix your shrimp and grits for my children. And then they can fix 'em for their children." The thought of her mama being gone brought tears to Bessie's eyes. *"It's like a piece of you that will live on and on."*

Mama shook her head. *"Child, you do have imaginations. Mother Mathilda is puttin' things in your head."*

Bessie couldn't argue. It was true. Her teacher had given her the idea of writing something about her parents. When she suggested a cookbook, Mother Mathilda had nodded her head. *"Yes'm,"* she'd said. *"I think that is a very worthy endeavor."*

Bessie wasn't completely sure what an endeavor was, but the way Mother Mathilda said it, it sounded like something very good.

Mama sighed and turned back to the stove.

Was she going to give Bessie the recipe or not? *"Mama, what are you stirrin' now?"*

"For your information, girl, I was soakin' grits all night long. Now I'm heatin' 'em up. You better get that notebook if you want my recipe." Portia turned around and frowned at Bessie while pointing her large wooden spoon at her. *"This is my own special secret recipe. You can't go showin' this to anyone else, you understand?"*

"But Mama, why not? That's the point. I'm savin' your cookin' so it will be shared down through the years. How is that gonna happen if no one can read it?" Bessie sighed deeply. *"Mother Mathilda wants to see it when it's done. Can I show it to her?"*

Mama was quiet for a moment. "All right. You can show Mother Mathilda. Lord knows she has put herself in danger for us. But after that, it stays in the family, okay?"

Bessie nodded. "I guess so, but I still don't understand."

Mama turned back once again to look at her. "I guess after gettin' my freedom, I jes want somethin' that's...mine. I came up with my shrimp and grits recipe, and I don't want everyone else makin' it. You probably can't understand that."

"I think I do. A little bit. I won't show it to anyone 'cept Mother Mathilda. And I will write somethin' inside that says this book can only be owned by someone in our family. I will give it to my daughter, and she can give it to hers." She took her notebook out of her schoolbag. After she opened it to a fresh page, she picked up her pencil and then looked up. "Is that all right, Mama?"

Mama smiled at her. "Yes'm. That will be jes fine," she said.

After a quick lunch at the office, Meredith and Julia headed to Mama Louise's kitchen. The restaurant was known for their quiche and it was hard not to order some, but they'd decided to only get coffee and dessert. The food budget was straining at the seams. Of course, even dessert at Mama Louise's was a little steep. Julia ordered a piece of hummingbird cake. It was a classic Southern dessert that had three layers and was filled with pineapples and bananas. Julia gulped at the price of fifteen dollars for one slice of cake, but when she took the first bite, she realized it was worth it.

"This might be one of the best things I've ever tasted," she whispered to Meredith.

But her partner was equally enthralled with her choice, sweet potato pie covered with thick whipped cream.

"Mmmm. Webb...nee...tall...er...home...," she tried to say after stuffing her mouth with pie.

"Meredith Bellefontaine," Julia hissed. "Quit talking with your mouth full. I can't understand a word you're saying."

Meredith blushed. She washed her food down with her coffee and then cleared her throat. "Sorry," she said quietly. "But this is delicious. I've never been here before, but I intend to come back. The rest of their menu must be incredible."

Julia nodded. "Beau and I have eaten here a couple of times, but since it was featured on *Cooking with Beverly,* the prices have skyrocketed. We still come once in a while, but neither of us wants to spend our life savings on a meal."

Meredith gazed around the dining room, and Julia glanced around too. Rather ostentatious but still attractive. Lots of red and gold. Red and gold patterned carpet, gold draperies, and large chandeliers created a rather royal atmosphere.

Meredith leaned in closer. "I was trying to say that this is a good time to speak to Jerome. There's hardly any business. He should be free."

"Seems strange," Julia said. "When Beau and I were here last you couldn't get in without a reservation."

"Well, it is the middle of the day."

Julia nodded. "I guess so, but it still seems odd."

Meredith looked past Julia as if wanting her to see something. Julia started to turn her head, but Meredith whispered, "Don't look."

Julia sighed. "I thought you were telling me to look."

Meredith just frowned at her. Julia was about to ask her what was going on when someone stepped up to their table. When Julia looked up she realized what Meredith had been trying to tell her. Laurel Hurst stood there, smiling at them. "I hope you're enjoying your desserts," she said with a wide smile. Then it seemed as if recognition came into her eyes. "You've been with us before," she said to Julia. "But I also saw both of you at the grits competition. Or should I say, the grits disaster."

"I'm Meredith Bellefontaine," Meredith said. Then she gestured toward Julia. "And this is Julia Foley. She and her husband have visited your fabulous restaurant many times before."

"Well, I'm so glad you came back," she said. "How is the food?"

"The best sweet potato pie I've ever tasted," Meredith said.

"And this hummingbird cake is exceptional," Julia added.

"But we're not here just to eat." Meredith put her fork down.

"No?" Laurel stood there, obviously waiting for Meredith to continue.

"Did you see the article in the paper accusing the cook from the Downhome Diner of substituting a jar of paprika with a jar of hot pepper during the contest?" Meredith asked.

Laurel's face turned red, "Yes, I did, and I believe he got it right. He's suing her for damages, isn't he?"

Julia shook her head. "No, the suit was dropped. There wasn't any evidence at all that Maribelle Sims or Charlene Jackson were involved in any way. We were hired by the Downhome Diner to find out what actually happened, even though the lawsuit was dismissed. They want their name cleared. A good reputation is important to a business."

"What do you mean, you were hired?" she asked. She lifted her chin and looked down on them with what Julia could only describe as *disdain*.

"Julia and I run an investigation agency," Meredith said.

Laurel crossed her arms over her chest. "But they made the only grits not garnished with that unearthly hot seasoning, isn't that right?"

Julia nodded. "Yes, but the diner has its own garnish. They use a smoked paprika blend. Their recipe is so special it's kept secret. They had no reason to use anything else."

Meredith cleared her throat then said, "Laurel, we'd like to talk to your chef, Jerome. It's rather important."

Laurel looked confused. "Jerome? May I ask why?"

"We have eyewitnesses who say they saw Jerome put the jar on the table," Meredith said. "We want to see if he confirms that."

"What are you saying? You think my chef purposely ruined the other dishes so… Well, so what? So he could win? That's ridiculous. Our dish was also spoiled with that stupid seasoning."

"We realize that," Julia said soothingly. "We're absolutely not accusing Jerome. We just want to find out why he put that bottle on the contestants' table and where and how he got it."

Laurel pointed her finger at them. "You'd better not try to say we were involved in ruining that contest. If you do, it won't be Charlene Jackson facing a lawsuit. It will be you."

Meredith took a deep breath and said, "As Julia mentioned, we're not accusing you or Jerome. In fact, with this incredible food, I can clearly see that there is no reason for you or Jerome to cheat. Your food and your reputation are exemplary. Above reproach."

Although Julia wondered if Meredith was laying it on a little thick, Laurel's expression relaxed some.

"Thank you," she said. She looked around her almost empty restaurant and then bent down closer to them. "You really should be talking to Sally Becker. She tried more than once to sabotage others in the contest."

"I don't understand," Julia said quietly as she wondered why they were keeping their voices down. No one else was anywhere near them.

Laurel sighed, bit her lip for a moment, and then said, "There were…*incidents* in the previous rounds. Like, two of the contestants were told that their entry fees were late. They weren't allowed to compete in the contest. Sally was in charge of receiving those entry fees. If you want to know who undermined the final round, you need to talk to her." Laurel straightened up. "I'll send Jerome out, but I'm telling you that he had nothing to do with what happened."

She turned on her heel and headed toward the kitchen.

Meredith looked at Julia. "Sally already told us about those late entries. I think Laurel's dislike of Sally is behind her accusations."

Julia understood Meredith's reasoning, but could there be some truth in Laurel's claims? Maybe Sally Becker hadn't been as forthcoming as they thought at first. Maybe she was the person they were looking for.

Chapter Fourteen

As SHE FINISHED HER DESSERT, Julia turned reasons over in her head as to why Laurel or Jerome would purposely ruin their own dish. It was obvious that Jerome was a master chef. He had every chance of winning the grits contest. But as she gazed around the almost empty restaurant, she began to wonder if the incident was a way to gain attention. Bring more customers to the restaurant. If that was the intention, it obviously wasn't working.

She watched as Jerome came out of the kitchen. He was a small man with a large nose and a handlebar mustache. Not something most men would wear, but it was his signature. Many times when referring to him in advertisements, instead of using his picture next to his name, there was just a picture of a handlebar mustache.

As he approached the table, he didn't look happy. Even though he wasn't a large person, his strong personality made up for his diminutive stature. He had the ability to strike trepidation into the hearts of those who opposed him. There had been rumors for quite some time that diners rarely sent food back to the kitchen at Mama Louise's due to Jerome's temper. Julia had at one time wondered why Laurel kept him on. But then she tasted his food and discovered the answer to that particular mystery.

"I understand you have some questions for me about that dreadful *grits contest.*" He spit out the words as if they were a bad taste in his mouth. "I didn't want anything to do with it, but Madame Laurel insisted."

"Why didn't you want to compete?" Meredith asked. "If your shrimp and grits are anything like these desserts, you certainly had an excellent chance of winning."

He sighed. "I was head chef for a superb restaurant in Paris. I came here because my daughter lives in Savannah. I accepted this position because I had to. But this *Southern* food. Well...it's so *déclassé.*"

Julia frowned. "There are several wonderful French restaurants in Savannah. Why didn't you apply for a job with them?"

He shrugged. "At the time I thought learning a new way of cooking would be a challenge. And at first it was. But now..." He let his words fade as he looked around, obviously making sure Laurel was out of earshot. "Let's return to your original reason for seeking me out. You want to know about the jar of ground ghost peppers?"

"Yes. We understand you put it on the table."

"Yes, but it wasn't filled with the ghost peppers when I was given the jar," Jerome said.

Julia was surprised by his response. "How do you know that?"

"Every morning I go for coffee at A Cup of Jo. When I was there Friday morning, before the contest, I was told that someone had left a letter and a package for me. The letter was from Ernie Prothro. He asked me to bring the paprika to the contest. He mentioned in the letter that the media would be covering the event and that the dishes would look better on television with a little color. He also said that the judges were partial to a topping of paprika as well. The letter said that the paprika was very mild and wouldn't change the taste of the completed dish."

"Didn't you find that odd?" Meredith asked.

Jerome hesitated. "*Oui*. A little. But Ernie Prothro is a very well-respected food critic." He seemed to suddenly stand just a little taller. "He was intelligent enough to give me an excellent review." He shrugged. "I trust his judgment. Besides, I've been on TV before, and adding things to food to give it color is done more than you might suspect. Paprika is one of the spices used to accomplish this. No one wants the food to look bland and unappetizing. The evening of the contest, I simply took the jar of paprika over to one of the tables as Ernie had requested. The only one there at that time was Cyrus Sharrah. I told him what the letter from Ernie said and asked him to tell the other contestants if he saw them before I did. Then, to be honest, I forgot all about it. I was too busy trying to get ready for the competition."

"Did you ask Ernie about the letter later?"

Jerome nodded. "Oui. After he and Beverly became ill. He said he didn't write the letter and he knew nothing about the paprika."

"Did you keep the letter?" Julia asked. "I'd like to see it."

"I'm sorry, but no. I threw it away. At the time I had no reason to keep it."

"You mentioned that you knew it was paprika when you picked it up," Julia said. "How did you know that?"

"I opened the lid and shook some into my palm. Then I tasted it. I have great respect for Ernie, but I needed to know that his opinion and mine were the same. It was definitely paprika. As Ernie said, it was very mild. That's why I decided to use it. It was light enough to add color to my dish without changing the taste." He shrugged. "If the television people wanted colorful food, I was happy to oblige. I wanted to win. Show these Southern cooks that I could beat them easily."

"So why do you think the other competitors used the paprika?" Meredith asked.

Jerome shrugged again. "I have no idea. I assumed it was because Cyrus shared the same message with the other contestants. Or maybe later, after I used it, the others followed my lead. Except for that woman from the Downhome Diner."

He practically spat out the words. It was pretty clear he didn't respect the diner. Probably not up to his lofty standards. Julia really didn't like Jerome Matheson. She found him stuffy and full of himself. But that didn't mean he'd done anything wrong. It felt as if every time she and Meredith got close to the truth, the road changed, leading them in a new direction. They needed to talk to Cyrus Sharrah.

"Thank you. We really appreciate your help," Meredith said.

Jerome hurried back to his kitchen as if even breathing the same air as anyone from Savannah was harmful.

"Wow," Julia said, keeping her voice low, "what a snob."

"Yes," Meredith replied, "but a very talented snob." She let loose a deep sigh. "I think I'm addicted to this pie."

"Do you believe him?" Julia asked.

"Yes, unfortunately I do. Why would he use the pepper unless he believed it was paprika? With that kind of ego, I can't imagine he would purposely ruin his grits during an event covered by the media."

"You're right," Julia said, "but I still don't trust him."

"I understand, but…" Meredith looked around the restaurant again. "I'm sorry, but it's really bugging me. Why aren't there more people here?"

Just then their waitress walked up to their table. "Can I get you more coffee, or anything else?"

Meredith shook her head. "We're fine, thanks, but could we see a dinner menu?"

The waitress walked over to a small table next to the hostess stand. Then she returned and handed Meredith a menu encased in black leather.

The waitress looked around before saying, "I'd invite you to come back, but after you look inside, I doubt we'll see you again." Without further explanation, she walked away.

"Wow," Meredith said, her eyes wide as she perused the menu. "I think I know why no one's here."

She passed the menu to Julia, who gasped at what she saw. "The prices are much higher than they were the last time Beau and I came here. They were steep then, but they've skyrocketed. The cheapest steak here is almost ninety dollars. And the salmon dinner is eighty." She gulped. "It comes with whatever vegetable they're serving that night, but salad or a baked potato is extra. Ten dollars." She shook her head and looked at Meredith. "We thought the lunch menu was ridiculous. But this is worse. Beau would never pay these prices, no matter how much we like the food."

"It seems other people agree with you. I'm no expert, but with all the exceptional restaurants in Savannah, most people aren't interested in spending this kind of money." The waitress who had given them the menu walked past them. Once again Meredith called her over.

"Can I help you?" she asked.

"These prices…," Julia said. "They're exceptionally high."

The waitress glanced around before leaning over to whisper, "We were highlighted on a local TV show. The woman on the show raved about us. Then the restaurant was reviewed in the paper. The food critic praised our food. Called us possibly the best restaurant in Savannah. Mrs. Hurst got it in her head that we should charge more. She kept raising the prices until they were way above any other restaurant in the city."

"So why doesn't Laurel lower them?" Meredith asked. "Surely she realizes what's happening."

The waitress sighed. "Fear."

"Fear of what?" Julia asked.

"Fear of losing Jerome. After the reviews he demanded a raise. Which she gave him. Now she's paying him a lot of money. More than most chefs in Savannah. She's afraid that if she lowers the menu prices, she might have to cut his salary. If she does that, he'll leave. He's made it abundantly clear that he believes the hype about him and won't work for less than what he's getting now." She sighed again. "I'm about ready to quit. I can't make tips from nonexistent customers. I hate to do it, because I've been here for six years. But I'm a single mom who lives paycheck to paycheck. This can't go on forever."

"But if Laurel lowered the prices, wouldn't she actually make more money since her traffic would increase?" Meredith asked.

"Yes, but it would take time to get the word out, and she's barely keeping her head above water now." She shrugged. "At least I think that's the reason."

"I'm sorry," Julia said. "Sounds like Laurel boxed herself in and now she can't find a way out." She smiled at the waitress. "Thank you for your candor. And for taking such good care of us."

"You're very welcome. I really hope to see you again sometime, but I won't be surprised if I don't." The waitress took a pad of paper from her pocket and tore off their bill. "Just leave it here, and I'll take care of it when you're ready. Are you sure I can't get you more coffee?"

Julia shook her head. "We need to be going, but thank you anyway."

As the waitress walked away, Meredith said, "This is really sad. I hope Laurel figures this out. I'd hate to see this wonderful restaurant close."

"I feel the same," Julia said. She reached into her purse and got her debit card, which she put inside the holder that contained the bill. A few minutes later the waitress picked it up and then came back with their receipt. After thanking them again, the waitress walked over to a table where an elderly couple had just been seated.

"I hope they have strong hearts," Meredith whispered. "Maybe we should warn them."

"Very funny." Julia took the receipt from the folder and added a large tip to the restaurant's copy. As she was doing this, Meredith pulled out her wallet and removed several bills.

"Put this in the folder," she said.

Julia smiled. "I just tipped her that same amount."

"Good," Meredith said. "I want to match it."

Julia didn't argue with her. She took the bills and slid them inside the folder. "I'm happy to help her, but this won't last long. She'll probably have to get a job somewhere else."

"Let's leave before she finds her tip. I don't want to embarrass her."

Julia stood up and followed Meredith out of the building. Jerome had given them another piece of the puzzle, but they still didn't have enough pieces to form a clear picture. There were three more people on their list to interview. Beverly Innes at Channel 6, Martin Seeger at the Seaside Grill, and Cyrus Sharrah. Would one of them have information that would lead the partners in the right direction? Or was this a case they couldn't solve?

Chapter Fifteen

BY THE TIME THEY GOT back to the office, it had started to rain again. Julia loved the rain. It made her feel peaceful. She would open her office curtains so she could enjoy this lovely shower while she worked.

She and Meredith parked and got out of the car. They hurried to the back door, trying not to get too wet. Julia had left her umbrella in her office, unaware that the weather would change. When they stepped inside, Carmen was waiting for them. The expression on her face stopped Julia in her tracks.

"Is something wrong?" she asked.

Carmen put her finger to her lips and shushed her before saying, "He's in your office. I didn't know what else to do. I thought about calling the cops."

Alarmed, Julia said, "Who are you talking about?"

"That man is here. You know, the man in the drawing. Prescott."

Meredith grabbed Julia's arm. "You can't see him. He's dangerous. Let's just call the police."

Although fear had rushed through her at the mention of his name, Julia wanted to hear what he had to say. If he really was innocent of the robberies that had sent him to prison, didn't she owe him something? Shouldn't she at least hear him out?

"I'm going to talk to him," she said. "You come with me, Meredith. And Carmen, if I buzz you and ask you to cancel my four o'clock appointment…"

"I call the cops."

"Yes, exactly."

"All right," Carmen said, "but I agree with Meredith. I don't have a good feeling about you meeting with this desperado."

Every time Carmen used that word, it reminded Julia of the song. Great. Now that melody would probably run through her head all day.

"Don't worry," she said. "I'll keep the door open." She looked at Meredith. "We can't assume there'll be a problem, can we? I'm not big on judging someone by their past. Even Grady Prescott."

"Where's your gun?" Meredith whispered.

"In my purse, but I have no plans to use it."

"Are you sure about this?"

"No, but it's what I need to do. I really would like to talk to him."

Meredith squared her shoulders. "Okay, let's go."

Julia took a deep breath and headed toward her office, praying as she walked. She asked God to protect her, Meredith, and Carmen—and to give her wisdom to know how to talk to Prescott.

When she stepped inside her office, she found him sitting in one of her Louis XV French chairs. She sat down behind her desk, and Meredith stood next to her.

"What can I do for you, Mr. Prescott?" she asked, trying to keep her voice steady.

"It's been a long time," he said. He smiled, but it didn't reach his eyes. "A long, long time. I spent over twenty years in prison because of you."

"If you were wrongly convicted, I'm sorry," Julia said. "But surely you realize that I didn't send you to prison. I only presented the facts of the case. The jury found you guilty and the judge sentenced you. She followed the law. We all did."

His eyebrows knit together in a frown. "There was no direct evidence that pointed to me as the person who robbed those people."

"Eyewitness testimony is considered evidence, Mr. Prescott."

"That old man made a mistake. Probably had dementia or something. You shouldn't have listened to him."

"The jury felt his testimony was credible."

"That jury was out to get me. They didn't like me."

Julia stood up. "I have no intention of going over the details of your trial. If you came here for that, it's time for you to leave." She refused to be intimidated by Grady Prescott. Instead of fear, she was beginning to feel anger. Why was he here? What did he want?

Prescott took a deep breath. After he let it out, he said, "All right, let's not talk about the trial. Let's talk about what you're doin' to me now."

Surprised, Julia asked, "What are you talking about?"

Anger flashed in his eyes. "You told the police I took your wallet the night of the grits contest. I didn't do no such thing."

"You ran into me, and later I found my wallet had been stolen from my jacket."

"I admit I bumped into you Friday night, but I didn't steal nothin'. You're hounding me. Since my case was overturned, you decided to spread lies about me so I'll get in trouble with the police."

Julia sat down again. "That's ridiculous. I only told them what happened. If you didn't steal my wallet you have nothing to worry about, do you?"

Prescott stood to his feet. "I just came here to tell you to leave me alone. I couldn't go back to Atlanta, because people there think I'm guilty of hurtin' that old man. So I came here to try to start over, and here you are. Tryin' to ruin my life. Again." His face flushed with anger. "Stay away from me," he said. "And quit lyin' to the police. I set them straight, told them what you were up to. I won't let you drive me away. I'll do whatever I have to do to stay here." He glared at her menacingly before walking out the door. Julia waited until she heard the front door close.

"I don't like him, Julia," Meredith said. "And I certainly don't trust him. You need to call the police and tell them about him. About his threats."

"But what if we were wrong, Meredith? Twenty years is a long time. If it's true, he has every right to be angry."

"First of all," Meredith said, "like you told him, you're not responsible for the sentence in Atlanta. A judge and a jury decided that. You only presented evidence." She frowned. "Julia, don't you find it odd that of all the people in this city he could run into, the chance that he'd bump into you is...astronomical?"

Julia did find it strange. But a lot of people had attended the grits contest. It had been well advertised. It wasn't completely impossible for Prescott to have come to River Street to see the event. And the crowd was tightly packed. Running into someone was almost a given. That it was Grady Prescott was weird...but was it impossible? "I don't know, Meredith. I'm really starting to doubt myself. I can't be sure that Prescott isn't telling the truth. I certainly didn't mean to bear false witness against anyone."

"Oh, Julia. You weren't bearing false witness." She paused for a moment. "Did you make up evidence? Did you lie about anything?"

"Of course not," Julia shot back. "I would never do that."

"Then why are you beating yourself up?"

Julia sighed. "I don't know. I guess just the idea of an innocent person spending years in prison—"

"But Julia, that wouldn't be your fault, even if it was true. You didn't convict him. A jury of his peers did, after listening to the evidence."

Julia shrugged. "But what about the inmate who confessed to the crimes? He seems credible."

Meredith snorted. "Oh yeah. The guy who isn't facing execution anymore. I'd certainly believe him."

"That bothers me too, but he was convincing enough to get Prescott's sentence overturned."

Meredith sat down on the corner of Julia's desk. "You've got to give this to the Lord, Julia. You can't go back and change things. Right now, there's no way to know the truth about Grady Prescott. So until we do, we need to concentrate on helping Charlene."

"You're right."

"Let's call Maggie Lu and ask her if she can join us for supper at the diner. It will give us a chance to tell Charlene what we know so far."

Julia smiled. "That sounds great. I'll call Beau and ask him if he wants to come."

"He's not going to be happy about Prescott coming to the office."

"I know, but there's nothing I can do about it."

Meredith glanced at her watch. "Hey, Beverly Innes should be wrapping up her afternoon show in a little while. Let's go down to the station and talk to her."

"I'm not sure they'll let us in," Julia said.

"The station manager was a client of Ron's. Helped him find out which one of his employees was giving news stories to a competitor before the station had a chance to report them. He's in Ron's debt. I'll bet I can wrangle us an invitation."

"Okay. I guess that would help me quit thinking about Prescott." Julia shook her head. "And that song. It keeps playing over and over in my mind. It's driving me crazy."

"What song?" Meredith asked.

"'Desperado' by the Eagles. Ever since Carmen called Prescott a desperado, I haven't been able to quit thinking about it."

Meredith's eyes widened. "Gee, thanks. Now it's going to get stuck in my mind too."

Julia laughed. "You're welcome. At least now we can share the pain."

Meredith grinned. "I'll make that call and let you know if we can talk to Beverly today."

After Meredith left for her own office, Julia turned her chair around and watched rivulets of rain stream down the windows. Taking Meredith's advice was easier said than done. She wanted to cast her care on the Lord, but something inside her needed to know if Prescott had been wrongly convicted. She prayed that God would help her find the truth, no matter how hard it would be to hear.

Chapter Sixteen

SURE ENOUGH, MEREDITH WAS ABLE to get them into the television station that afternoon. The station manager, Osgood Bronson, met them at the front desk. He was tall and thin with a receding hairline, which he tried to hide by combing his remaining hair forward. He smiled widely when he saw them come through the door.

"So glad to see you, Meredith," he said, walking toward them.

"You too, Osgood." She gestured toward Julia. "This is my friend and partner, Julia Foley."

Osgood stuck his hand out, and Julia shook it. "I heard you'd kept the detective agency open and were running it with someone." He let go of Julia's hand. "I was happy to hear that. Ron loved his work. I'm glad to hear it's continuing."

Meredith smiled at him. "I believe that's what he would have wanted."

"I do too. So, what's this about you wanting to talk to Beverly? You said on the phone it had something to do with what happened at the grits contest Friday night?"

"Yes," Meredith said. "We're trying to find out how the entries were compromised. I don't know if you're aware of this, but some people have been blaming friends of ours who had nothing whatsoever to do with it."

"Are you talking about the owner and the chef at the Down-home Diner?" he asked.

"Yes. Because their dish wasn't tampered with, some people believe they were responsible for what happened."

Osgood frowned. "Surely you don't suspect Beverly of anything, do you?"

"Absolutely not," Meredith said. "We're just hoping she might have noticed something that night. Maybe she can point us in the right direction."

He nodded. "Why don't you come with me? I'll take you into the studio so you can watch the last few minutes of her show. You have to be very quiet though. No talking until she's finished."

Meredith made a zipping motion with her fingers over her mouth. "Not a word."

Osgood chuckled. "Follow me, ladies."

They walked through the large lobby and down a hall until they reached a set of double doors. A lighted sign over the doors read ON AIR.

Osgood quietly opened one of the doors and ushered them inside. The studio was dark except for one area. Lights on poles illuminated Beverly's set while two cameras were focused on her.

Osgood led them to some chairs behind the cameras. They sat down, and Osgood stood behind them. Over to one side a small crowd of people watched Beverly. They had to be the studio audience. Beverly was cooking something. Julia wasn't sure what it was, but Beverly was effusive and fun to watch. After a few minutes Julia realized Beverly was making Hoppin' John, a Southern dish made with black-eyed peas, rice, bacon, and several special seasonings. It smelled wonderful. When Beverly showed the finished dish, one that had obviously been made earlier, the audience cheered. She took some small bowls that sat on the island and began to fill them. Then she grabbed some spoons. A man who'd been standing nearby, but out of the camera's view, ran over and began to carry the bowls and spoons to the audience that was obviously excited to taste Beverly's dish. The cameras panned their way, and their expressions made it clear it was a big hit. After the audience had been served, Beverly ended the show with her signature line, "Nothin' says lovin' like somethin' from my oven!" The audience cheered again. When they stopped, Beverly said, "Tomorrow I'll show you how to make the best chicken-fried steaks you've ever tasted! Thanks for visiting my kitchen, Savannah! See you tomorrow!"

She smiled and waved. Then the sign over the doors that said On Air turned off and the lights in the studio came up. The man who had handed out the bowls hurried over to Beverly and removed the small microphone that was attached to her blouse. After that, he went over to thank the audience members for coming and picked up their bowls and spoons.

Julia watched as Beverly walked over to the audience and spoke to each one of them before they were shown the exit. She seemed to enjoy what she did. Her curly brown hair was pulled back from her face and secured with rhinestone clips. Her tan slacks and turquoise blouse made her look casual but approachable. Osgood waited until the audience was gone and then guided her to where Julia and Meredith waited.

"Beverly," he said. "These ladies would like to talk to you. This is Meredith Bellefontaine. I was friends with her husband, Ron, before he passed away."

"Oh, I'm so sorry," Beverly said, compassion in her hazel eyes.

"Thank you," Meredith said. "I really enjoyed your show."

Beverly smiled. "Thank you. I appreciate that."

"And this is Julia Foley," Osgood continued. "They run a detective agency."

Julia smiled. "We like to call it an investigation agency. We don't really see ourselves as *detectives*. That word brings to mind Sherlock Holmes or Monk."

Beverly laughed. "I like that." She paused and looked back and forth between Julia and Meredith. "I've seen you before, but I'm not sure where."

"We were at the grits contest Friday night," Meredith said. "Could that be it?"

Beverly snapped her fingers. "Yes." She shook her head. "Not my finest hour. That poor Barbie Patzweaver on Channel 4. I feel so bad about what happened."

"It wasn't your fault," Julia said.

Beverly sighed. "I know, but I just keep thinking that if only I'd aimed away from her, I wouldn't have ruined that nice pantsuit of hers."

Julia was impressed by Beverly's concern for Barbie. They worked for competing television stations, and having compassion for Barbie probably wasn't the easiest thing in the world.

"I called over there and asked to speak to her, but she wouldn't take my call." Beverly clucked her tongue. "I don't blame her, I guess. But I'd really like to make it up to her."

"I've told her she should just let it go," Osgood said, "but she hasn't been able to."

A woman standing on the other side of the studio called out Osgood's name.

"You three talk," he said. "I need to speak to our producer." He pointed at Meredith. "See me before you go, okay?"

"I will," Meredith said.

"Let's sit down over here," Beverly said, pointing to a table and chairs not far from the set. "How about a bowl of Hoppin' John? It's still hot."

"Sounds wonderful," Meredith said.

"You ladies sit down. I'll be right back."

Julia thanked her and followed Meredith over to the table, where they sat down to wait for Beverly.

"Boy, that woman is something else," Julia said under her breath. "The difference between her and Barbie is like night and day."

Meredith nodded. "Maybe Barbie's still upset about being named after a plastic doll."

Julia giggled. "That would tend to upset a person. Hard to live up to the real Barbie. Impossible measurements and all."

This time Meredith laughed. "Seriously," she said, shaking her head, "do you remember where Beverly was the night of the contest?"

"Obviously too close to Barbie," Julia said. "That would mean she was at the end of the table. Before that..." Julia tried to remember. "You know, I don't remember seeing her until right before the judging. I could have missed her because I was watching Maribelle, but I really think I would have noticed her."

"You're right. I don't remember seeing her either," Meredith said slowly.

Julia saw Beverly coming toward them with a tray in her hands. Once she reached the table, she put it down and handed each of them a bowl. Then she picked up soup spoons and napkins from the tray.

"How about something to drink?" she asked. "Hoppin' John can be a little spicy. Our vending machine has different kinds of soda, iced tea, and water."

"You sit down," Julia said. "You've been on your feet for a while. I'll get us something to drink. What would you like, Beverly?"

"Why, thank you, honey," Beverly said with a smile. "I have to admit that my feet are a little sore." She thought for a moment. "I'd love a Diet Dr Pepper."

Julia grinned. "A woman after my own heart." She looked at Meredith.

"Just some water. Thanks, Julia."

Julia nodded and headed for the vending machine. Her jaunt for beverages gave her a chance to look over the studio a little more closely. She found it interesting that the set was so well designed, but rest of the studio was plain. Off-white walls, cement floors. It reminded her of a garage. She had the vending machine in sight, but before she got there a man stepped up to it and put some money in. She waited behind him. When he had his selection in hand, he turned around and almost ran into Julia.

"Sorry," he said. "I didn't see you."

"That's okay. No damage done."

Rather than walking away, he gave a brief nod toward the table where Meredith and Beverly sat. "You're a friend of Beverly's?"

"No. I just met her a few minutes ago. We're here to ask her some questions about the grits contest Friday night."

The man snickered. "Watching her majesty lose her lunch was one of the funniest things I've seen in a long time. It was caught on tape, you know. One of the other stagehands recorded it on his phone and plays it over and over on a continuous loop. Hysterical."

"It sounds like you don't like Beverly," Julia said, her voice low. "She seems very nice."

"That's her act. The truth is she's meaner than a rattlesnake to people like me. The *little people* who can't help her. If she's nice to you, I'd be worried. She probably wants something." He shrugged. "Par for the course in television. Their egos end up bigger than their talent. You get used to it after a while." He looked around the room. "I'd appreciate it if you kept this between you and me. Mr. Bronson is pretty protective of her."

"I won't repeat it to anyone here," Julia said. "Thanks for the heads-up."

"You're welcome."

The man walked away, and Julia turned back to the vending machine. So Beverly Innes wasn't who she appeared to be. But did her personality have anything to do with their case? Julia didn't see how it could. As she purchased their drinks, she tried to forget the disgruntled man's comments for now.

Chapter Seventeen

Once she'd given Beverly and Meredith their drinks, Julia opened her bottle of Diet Dr Pepper and then took a bite from the bowl Beverly had given her. It was absolutely delicious, though a bit spicy, as Beverly had warned them.

"This is wonderful," she told Beverly. "Does the station post your recipes on their website?"

"Yes, they do," she said. "And they're easy to print if you'd like one. So you think you might make this at home?"

Julia nodded. "Without a doubt. My husband will love this." She swung her gaze around the studio. "How long have you been doing this?"

"I had a cooking show in Atlanta before coming here," Beverly said. "Four years there and seven here. I love it. Can't imagine doing anything else."

"I really do enjoy your show," Meredith said. "I've made several of your dishes. Ron loved your fried chicken recipe."

"You're too kind." Beverly took a drink before saying, "So what is it you wanted to talk to me about?"

"We're investigating what happened Friday night," Julia said. "There have been accusations that our friend Charlene Jackson, who owns the Downhome Diner, had something to do with putting that jar of hot pepper on the table. We know it's not true, but as I'm sure you can understand, Charlene wants to find out what really happened so her name can be cleared."

"Hot pepper? What kind of pepper?"

"Ground ghost peppers," Meredith said.

Beverly shook her head. "That's awful. That stuff is unbelievably hot. I thought the top of my head was coming off."

"Are you doing okay now?" Julia asked.

"Yes, but the side effects stayed with me for a couple of days. I was beginning to wonder if I would ever get my sense of taste back."

"I'm so sorry," Meredith said. "We'd really like to find out who did this. Someone should be held responsible."

"You're wondering if I noticed anything that might help you?"

"Exactly," Meredith said. "Several people have told us that Jerome Matheson from Mama Louise's was the one responsible for making the seasoning available, but he told us he truly believed it was paprika and that Ernie Prothro was the one who suggested they use it to add some color to their dishes."

Beverly frowned. "I wish I could help you, but I was late getting to the contest Friday night. Arrived right before the competition began." She paused and looked away for a moment. "I did see the jar at the end of the contest, but to be honest, I didn't think anything about it. It was sitting next to one of the contestant's hot plates. I assumed it belonged to them. I had no idea it had been passed around. Not until later, anyway." She stopped for a moment, and her eyes narrowed. "You know, now that I think about it, I did notice one other thing."

"What's that?" Julia asked, hoping it would be something that would help them.

"While everyone was running around, trying to help us, the jar disappeared. I didn't think much about it at the time, but later, when someone told me that whatever was in it made me sick, I looked for it. It was gone. Then, as I was being treated by the paramedics, I realized it was back. I thought that was odd, and I told one of the police officers about it. He immediately put the bottle into an evidence bag and took it to his car. Later I heard that the police asked our cameraman for his film from that night." Beverly shrugged. "That's all I know. In fact, I have no idea if the police have the footage or if it helped them at all. I'm sorry I can't tell you more. I've been so busy with the show."

Julia and Meredith looked at each other. "Can you give us the name of the cameraman the police talked to?" Meredith asked.

Beverly nodded. "Lyndon Perry. He's still here. Would you like me to introduce you?"

"That would be great," Julia said. "Maybe he filmed something that will help us."

"I hope so. I really do." Beverly finished her Diet Dr Pepper and stood to her feet. "You two ladies stay here. I'll find Lyndon and send him over to talk to you."

"Thank you so much for your help," Meredith said. "It was so nice to finally meet you."

Beverly smiled. "You too." She reached into the pocket of her slacks and pulled out a card. Then she picked up a pen from the table and scribbled something on the back of the card. "Here's my personal email address," she said, handing it to Julia. "When you try this dish at home, let me know what your husband has to say. I love to hear that people are enjoying my recipes."

"I appreciate that," Julia said. "I'll certainly contact you."

"I look forward to it." Beverly turned and walked away.

"What if someone filmed Maribelle taking that jar off the table?" Julia whispered to Meredith. "People may see that as proof she tampered with it."

"If Beverly was talking about Maribelle, we'll deal with it. But we need to find out. Besides, why would she show us that she had taken it if she was guilty of tampering with it? Doesn't make sense."

"I hope you're right. By the way, did you see me talking to a guy at the vending machine?" Julia asked.

Meredith nodded.

"He can't stand Beverly. Called her a rattlesnake. Told me if she was nice to us, we should worry."

Meredith frowned. "Oh, Julia, she seems all right. Maybe he's just a disgruntled employee. And even if what he said is true, which I doubt, he shouldn't be saying something like that to a stranger. It's inappropriate."

"Yeah, maybe," Julia said slowly. "But what if it's true? What if Beverly knows more than she's saying and she's trying to make us think she's sincere?"

Meredith sighed. "We can't be suspicious of everyone. Let's see what the cameraman has to say and take it from there."

Julia hated being so negative, but she couldn't just dismiss the man's words about Beverly.

"I heard you wanted to talk to me."

Julia jumped at the man's voice behind her. She turned around and looked up into the face of the man she'd spoken to at the vending machine.

"Hello again," Julia said with a smile.

"Oh, hey," he said. "Beverly said you have some questions about that grits contest?"

"Yes we do," Meredith said. "Have a seat."

"Beverly said you have some film from Friday night?" Julia asked as Lyndon sat down.

He nodded. "I was filming the contest and of course, Beverly, when things went south. I should have turned off the camera, but in the confusion, I left it on. Recorded several minutes after the...incident. When I realized the camera was still on I immediately turned it off."

"Beverly told us you gave the footage to the police. Is that right?"

"Yeah. To be honest, I don't see why this is so important. I mean, no one died or even got all that sick."

"I understand," Julia said, "but we're friends with the woman who owns the Downhome Diner. They were the only ones who didn't use the pepper. It makes it look as if they had something to do with sabotaging the other contestants. We're trying to clear their names."

"Did your camera pick up anything unusual?" Meredith asked.

Lyndon nodded. "Yes, and the police were interested in what I accidentally filmed."

Meredith cleared her throat. Julia could tell she was nervous. It was possible that whatever Lyndon caught on film could be important. "Is there any way we can see what you showed the police?"

Lyndon shrugged and pulled his phone out of his pocket. "I uploaded it to my phone." He swiped the screen a few times and then placed the phone on the table. Julia reached for it, and Meredith scooted closer to her. Julia pressed the arrow on the video and it began to play. Beverly popped up. Lyndon was placing the mic on her jacket. Then he worked on camera settings. When he got what he wanted Julia could hear him telling Beverly he was going to film the introduction of the contest, then the camera would swing to her.

"Just be sure to let me know when you do that," she said, her tone curt.

Julia heard Lyndon say, "I will."

Just a few seconds later Barbie made her way to the judging table. She waited until someone notified her that it was time to start. Her over-the-top smile appeared, and she began to introduce the contest and the contestants.

Julia couldn't help sighing. They'd seen this before. It wasn't anything new. Finally, the competition got to the place where the judges sampled the grits. Julia and Meredith watched carefully. Julia had already spotted the jar of paprika. The contestants had obviously already sprinkled the offensive spice on their food.

As the judges began to taste the food, Julia steeled herself for what was coming. Sure enough, there it was—Beverly throwing up all over Barbie. The look on Barbie's face was priceless. Unbelief mixed with horror. As the camera continued to roll, those gathered around the table for the contest reacted to the situation, most of them moving away.

A short time later Julia was horrified to see Maribelle grab the jar and walk away. A few minutes later, she returned and put the jar back on the table. Then she walked away.

Julia exchanged a glance with Meredith. It was there, and they couldn't do anything about it. But Maribelle hadn't done anything wrong, and Julia was determined to defend her innocence.

Then the video ended. Julia started to push the phone back to Lyndon when Meredith said. "Wait a minute. Can you play that again? It went by so quickly, I just want to see it again."

Julia touched the screen to allow the film to start over.

Once again they watched as Maribelle picked up the jar.

"Is this what you were looking for?" Lyndon asked.

"Yes, and no," Julia said. "We already knew about this. Our friend took the jar and brought it to us after the judges became ill. We examined the contents and suspected the jar contained ground ghost peppers. Once we were through with it, she took it back. I have to wonder what the police will make out of this though."

Lyndon shrugged. "If she'd taken it and kept it, that would be a problem. But she returned it to the table. Besides, the damage had already been done. What could she possibly be doing that would be of importance to the police? I wouldn't worry."

Julia wondered if the police would draw the same conclusion.

Chapter Eighteen

LYNDON PUSHED HIS CHAIR BACK and stood up. "Is there anything else I can do for you? I need to get to work."

"Yes," Meredith said. She took a card from her purse. "Could you send that video to me? We'd like to look it over a little more closely."

Lyndon hesitated. "I'm not sure."

"This is just for our own use," Julia said. "We're the only ones who will watch it. We just want to make sure we're seeing the same thing the police are. Once we figure out what happened we'll delete it. Does that help?"

Lyndon nodded slowly. "I guess so. Just be careful. I don't want to get in trouble for sharing something I'm not supposed to."

"You won't," Meredith said. "We just want to make sure there's nothing on the footage that we might have missed."

"Okay." Lyndon took the card with Meredith's email address and forwarded the video to her. Julia wasn't sure how much help it was actually going to be. She hadn't seen anything that they didn't already know. They thanked Lyndon for his help, and he walked away.

"Let's get going," Meredith said. "I really do want to go over this more closely. Maybe we'll see something that will help us solve this thing."

"I guess," Julia said, "but all I saw was Maribelle picking up the jar. I sure hope this doesn't cause her problems. I wish she'd just left it on the table.

Meredith shrugged. "I do too, but it's too late to change that."

"Hey, why don't you call Quin and see if he wants to join us for supper at the diner?"

Meredith nodded. "I will. He'd probably enjoy that."

"Let's go back to the office and view that footage again. Then we'll get ready for tonight, okay?"

"Sounds good."

When they got to the agency it was close to four o'clock. They went to the conference room, where Meredith got out her laptop and set it up on the table. Julia turned off the light and closed the drapes so they could see the video clearly.

Meredith played it once and then again, advancing the footage slowly, but they didn't notice anything unusual.

"Let's get ready for dinner," Meredith said. "Tomorrow we'll visit the coin shop and see if we can find out something helpful from them."

"I hope they'll talk to us. They may feel we have no right to ask them questions, and it's possible the police won't appreciate us involving ourselves in their case."

Meredith shrugged. "Hey, if we don't irritate them from time to time, we aren't doing our jobs."

Julia laughed. "I guess you're right." She glanced at the clock. "Want to meet at the diner at seven? That'll give us some time to rest and get ready to eat again."

"That sounds great. I'll call Quin now."

Meredith got up and went to her office. Julia was glad Meredith had found Quin. He'd been a corporate attorney but now owned his own firm and only took cases that interested him.

Julia felt that Quin was good for Meredith. He'd lost his wife, Andrea, a few years back, so he understood the path of grief that had to be walked by those who'd had their life ripped in two and their dreams for the future dashed. After knowing Quin for a while, Meredith seemed much happier now. It was clear she still missed Ron, but Julia could see the signs of healing. She was glad that Meredith and Quin were taking it slow. Julia had friends who'd lost a spouse and married again too quickly, hoping it would fill the void they felt. But in most cases it had turned out to be a mistake. Making a lifelong commitment to someone because of loneliness usually ended in disappointment and hurt. Quin and Meredith's approach was wise, and Julia was hopeful that their cautious approach would pay off when the time was right.

She sighed and ran the video once more. This time her attention wandered from the contestants and judges and focused on the crowd. She gasped when she saw something she and Meredith had missed. Standing to the side of the table, mixed in with the crowd, was Grady Prescott.

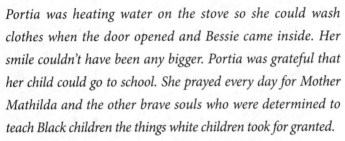

January 1872

Portia was heating water on the stove so she could wash clothes when the door opened and Bessie came inside. Her smile couldn't have been any bigger. Portia was grateful that her child could go to school. She prayed every day for Mother Mathilda and the other brave souls who were determined to teach Black children the things white children took for granted.

"What you smilin' about, child?" she asked.

"I showed Mother Mathilda the book," Bessie said, breathing heavily. She'd obviously run all the way home.

"And what did she say?" Portia asked.

Bessie sat down at the table and took a deep breath. "She said it was somethin' special. That now you would live forever, Mama."

Portia turned around and frowned at her daughter. "No one lives forever, girl. You know that."

"But remember what we talked about? That the things we do in life go on after we're gone?" Bessie set her books on the table and pulled the pages with Portia's recipes out of the stack. They'd been bound together between leather covers.

"Where did you get those?" Portia asked, leaving the sink and coming over to stroke the leather.

"Mother Mathilda gave them to me. She said the book deserved the best. That it would last longer with nice, strong covers. Ain't...aren't they lovely, Mama?"

Bessie beamed with pride, and Portia felt her eyes fill with tears.

"Why you cryin', Mama?" Bessie asked, her smile fading and her face showing her concern.

"I'm not sad, child. I'm just so proud of you."

"Thank you, Mama." Bessie patted the cover of the cookbook. "Now somethin' of you will be left behind for other people. It's a wonderful thing, ain't...isn't it?"

"Oh, Bessie Mae. Don't you realize that the most special thing I'm leavin' behind is you?"

This time Bessie's eyes overflowed with tears. "I love you, Mama," she said.

"And I love you too, Bessie Mae," Portia said, wiping her wet cheeks with her apron.

Chapter Nineteen

BEAU AND JULIA ARRIVED AT the Downhome Diner a little before seven. Julia had noticed Beau glancing in the rearview mirror and looking around as they drove. He was on edge because of Grady Prescott. Julia was certain Prescott had other things on his mind besides her, but she kept asking herself why had he ended up in Savannah. Why hadn't he just stayed in Atlanta? Maybe he was telling the truth. Maybe he needed a new location where he could start his life over again. But why did it have to be here? One of the voices in her head told her that Prescott was guilty, and that the confession in prison from Gerald Turano was bought and paid for with a promise of escaping the death penalty. But another voice asked if there was any possibility she had been wrong. The thought tortured her. Try as she might, she just couldn't shake it.

Beau parked, and they got out and went inside. Julia noticed Beau looking around as they walked to the entrance of the diner, but she pretended not to. Although the clouds had moved out, the scent of rain was still in the air. Usually Julia would have enjoyed this, but right now all she could think about was Beau. This situation was putting a lot of pressure on her husband, whose heart didn't need the stress.

She'd called Meredith and told her about seeing Prescott near the tables where the food was prepared at the contest. Meredith didn't like knowing Prescott was that close, but there wasn't any evidence that he'd tampered with anything. Julia was beginning to wonder if he'd followed her there. Maybe he was just trying to intimidate her and had nothing to do with what happened that night. As long as he didn't threaten her or touch her physically, he had the freedom to go wherever he wanted. Perhaps he was simply letting her know that he was free. Wanting her to feel that he had won some kind of victory over her. But no matter what the DA's office in Atlanta said, Julia found it hard to see him above suspicion.

Julia and Meredith agreed not to talk about Grady Prescott at dinner. They wanted the focus to be on Charlene and the diner.

Meredith and Quin were already at the restaurant, sitting at a table in the back. As Julia and Beau headed their way, Julia noticed the diner wasn't as busy as usual. True, it was Tuesday night, not a big night for restaurants, but she'd been here many times, and the thin crowd was definitely unusual.

"We just got here," Meredith said as they approached the table. "Isn't this awful? Where is everyone?"

Julia and Beau sat down. "Well, it is Tuesday…," Julia said.

"Still, this doesn't seem right."

"Good to see you, Quin," Beau said.

"You too," he responded.

"Have you seen Charlene?" Julia asked Meredith.

She shook her head. "Not yet."

As soon as the words left Meredith's mouth, Charlene walked out of the kitchen. She noticed them immediately and waved. After saying something to one of the waitresses, she came over to their table.

"Good to see you," she said with a smile.

"Not a big crowd tonight," Meredith said.

Charlene nodded. "It's been this way since that article in the paper on Saturday. Do people think we're going to poison them if they eat here?"

"Your regular customers won't believe that," Julia said.

Charlene shrugged. "Some of them haven't shown up either. Just because someone likes your food, it doesn't mean they *know* you. Or trust you."

Quin shook his head. "You got involved with the grits contest as a way to build your business. It seems to have backfired."

"Ernie Prothro said the newspaper would print a correction, but I haven't seen it yet."

"Let me contact him," Quin said. "Maybe the threat of a suit for slander will make things move faster."

"That would be wonderful, Quin," Julia said. She didn't miss the look Meredith gave him. She couldn't help but smile.

"Thank you," Charlene said. "I really appreciate that."

The door to the diner opened, and Maggie Lu walked in. Julia waved her over.

"My goodness," Maggie Lu said. "So happy to see you all. Thanks for asking me to join you." She pulled out the remaining chair at the table and sat down.

"I was telling them that we hadn't seen any kind of retraction from that story in the paper," Charlene said. "But Quin is offering to contact Ernie Prothro and give him a little nudge. Maybe the fear of a lawsuit will get things moving a little faster."

"Sounds like a great idea to me," Maggie Lu said with a sigh. "Thank you, Quin."

"You're welcome," he said.

Charlene put her hands on her hips. "And I don't care what you all say, when all of this is over, you both get a meal on the house, whatever you want." She took her pad out of her apron pocket. "Now, what will you have?" she asked.

Quin grinned at her. "I've been hearing so much about your famous shrimp and grits, I've got to try it."

Meredith laughed. "I love your shrimp and grits. I'll take that too."

Beau smiled at Julia. "Are we going to let these two make us look bad?"

"Absolutely not," Julia said. "Shrimp and grits."

Maggie Lu gave an exaggerated sigh. "Well, for goodness' sake. I don't want to be the odd man out. I'll go along with the group, sweetie."

Charlene chuckled. "At least I won't have to write that down." She pointed at Julia. "I know you want Diet Dr Pepper. How about everyone else?"

After getting their drink orders, Charlene started back toward the kitchen, but before she got too far, Maggie Lu called out, "And by the way, Charlene. Will you please tell Maribelle to leave the hot pepper off mine?"

There was a brief silence before everyone at the table broke out laughing. Julia looked around the restaurant and was tickled to see other customers laugh along with them.

Charlene grinned at her mother and shook her finger at her before entering the kitchen.

"Might as well laugh instead of cry," Maggie Lu said. "This certainly has been a tough few days. But with every trial that comes, blessing comes too."

"And what's the blessing with this trial?" Meredith asked.

"The blessing is that something like this teaches you who your real friends are. And I know some of our most precious friends are sitting at this table."

Julia blinked away the tears that filled her eyes. These people really were special to her, and she was blessed to have them in her life.

"We actually have a suspect, Maggie Lu," Julia said. "We just haven't figured out how to link him to what happened. But we will." She told Maggie Lu about Prescott bumping into her Friday night and taking her wallet.

"So you think this man is connected somehow?"

Julia nodded. "Too big of a coincidence for me. He was there for a reason."

"Granny Luv used to say that when somethin' stinks and the dog looks guilty, it doesn't make sense to blame the cat for the pile of poo on the floor."

Everyone at the table laughed. "That says it pretty well," Julia said.

"By the way," Maggie Lu said, "have I ever told you where our recipe for shrimp and grits comes from?"

"I don't believe so," Julia said. "I think you may have mentioned that it was passed down in your family."

Maggie Lu smiled. "Yes. My brother Benny was married to a woman named Clementine. Her great-great grandmother, Bessie Goodman-Evans, put together a cookbook with the help of a woman named Mathilda Beasley. Back then it was against the law to educate Black children, but Mathilda didn't care. She believed that educated

Black children would have a much better chance to succeed in the world. Mother Mathilda, as she was called, asked her students to write about someone they admired. Bessie picked her mother. Portia Goodman was a wife and mother. Black women didn't have a lot of choices back then, but Portia wasn't the kind of person to feel slighted. She loved her family. Bessie decided that if she saved her mother's recipes, she would be preserving part of Portia." Maggie Lu laughed lightly. "The problem was that Portia never measured anything. Didn't even know how. So Mathilda stepped in with her own measuring cups and spoons. Bessie helped Portia figure out how to cook with them. Clementine told me Portia wasn't too crazy about it, but she went along for Bessie's sake.

"Portia made Bessie swear that the book would stay in the family. So before she died, Clementine gave the book to Granny Luv. It was supposed to go to Clementine and Benny's son, Luke, when he was older, but when he took off and we lost touch, Granny Luv gave it to me, and I eventually gave it to Charlene. Several of the dishes she cooks come from that book. Shrimp and grits is only one of them." She smiled. "Not long after Granny Luv gave it to me, I took it to a professional who restored it and encased the pages in plastic so they would last."

"Oh, Maggie Lu," Julia said. "That's lovely. How do you know so much about Portia and Bessie?"

"Bessie wrote the story down, which was also passed along through the family. Bessie admired her mother immensely. Portia was a strong woman who taught her children to be resilient. To always believe that God had a purpose for them and that they were on the earth for a reason. Bessie went on to be a teacher who impacted the lives of many, many students.

"What a wonderful story," Meredith said, her eyes full of tears.

"Bessie made certain her mother would live on in the hearts of people after she passed away." Maggie Lu blinked away tears. "I suppose that's something we all want. Granny Luv taught me that we all leave fingerprints behind us. Some of us put our hands to negative things, but others touch hearts and lives with love and inspiration. Those fingerprints will go on and on. Portia taught her children how to love, and that lesson has continued down through our family."

"So the shrimp and grits we're eating tonight are courtesy of a special woman who lived in the 1800s," Quin said. "That's really something. I wonder how many things we take for granted without realizing why we have them and who brought them to us."

"Exactly," Maggie Lu said. "History is important. We can't appreciate what people have fought to give us unless we take a moment to look back and understand." She smiled. "The actual cookbook isn't here now, but next time you all come, I'll bring it so you can see it yourselves."

"That would be wonderful, Maggie Lu," Meredith said. "I'd love to see it."

Everyone at the table voiced their agreement. A moment later, Charlene came out with a tray and put five servings of shrimp and grits on the table.

"This looks delicious," Quin said.

"You'll love it," Julia said with a smile.

Beau offered to say grace. When he finished everyone dug in.

"This is so good," Quin said. "And very different."

"It's a traditional Southern recipe," Maggie Lu said, "but Charlene uses a special smoked paprika for seasoning."

A few minutes later, Charlene came back to the table. "How is everything?" she asked.

"This might be one of the best things I've ever put in my mouth," Quin said. "I can't believe you wouldn't have won that contest if it hadn't been sabotaged."

"Thank you," Charlene said. "I think we had a chance. I worked with several other restaurants to put the event together. I was so excited about it." She shook her head. "All for nothing now."

"Don't worry, Charlene," Julia said. "We'll find out who was behind this. Everything will be all right."

As she tried to encourage Charlene, Julia wondered if she would be able to keep that promise.

Chapter Twenty

AFTER WALKING IN THE BACK door of the agency Wednesday morning, Julia was on her way to her office when she heard Carmen call her name. She turned to see Carmen walking toward her.

"Officer Frett is here," she said softly. "He's waiting in reception."

"Thanks." Why was he here? If he wanted to talk to her, why didn't he just call? She headed to her office. What was so important that he'd come in person? After she got settled, she called Carmen and asked her to show Officer Frett to her office. A few moments later he walked in. She gestured to the chairs in front of her desk.

"Officer Frett, what can I do for you?" she asked.

"I have some news that I felt should be shared in person," he said. "I hope I'm not interrupting you?"

"No, of course not."

"Last night we arrested the man who stole your wallet."

"You arrested Grady Prescott?" Julia asked, surprised but happy at the news.

"No, ma'am," he said. He reached into his jacket pocket and pulled out a notebook. "The person who took your wallet is Cliff Randolph. He's a petty thief who's been in trouble before."

"But…but Grady Prescott took my wallet. My friend saw him do it."

Officer Frett frowned. "What do you mean she *saw* him do it? Did she actually observe him reach into your jacket and pull out your wallet?"

Julia faltered for a moment. She knew how important it was to be accurate when reporting a crime. Why had she said that? "Well, no. I misspoke, I guess. But she did see him bump into me, and a short time later I discovered that my wallet was gone."

"So the only thing you can really say about Mr. Prescott is that he ran into you, isn't that correct?"

"Yes, but as you know, pickpockets use that technique to steal wallets. I was convinced Grady Prescott took mine."

"Well, Mr. Randolph has confessed to the crime. He says he found your wallet in the parking lot, not far from the contest area. He took the money and the credit cards. Then he threw it toward a dumpster nearby. He tried to use one of the cards at Mr. Andre's. The clerk he spoke to has identified him as the man who attempted to buy something there with your stolen card." Officer Frett wrote something in his notebook. "Where were you parked, Mrs. Foley?"

Julia described the area where Meredith had parked her car.

"Mr. Randolph contends that he discovered your wallet on the ground not far from that same location. Couldn't you have accidentally dropped it after you got out of the car?"

"What time did he find it?"

"It was after the contest ended," the officer said, "but that doesn't prove anything. It could have been there the entire time."

Julia tried to contain her irritation. This wasn't the officer's fault. He was simply trying to do his job, but something strange was going on. She was certain Prescott was behind it.

"So you think it's just a coincidence that Grady Prescott, a man I prosecuted and helped to send to prison in Atlanta, shows up at the grits contest in Savannah where I happen to be and just a little later bumps into me around the same time my wallet went missing?"

"Mrs. Foley, I'm asking you if it's at all possible that you might have dropped your wallet in the parking lot after getting out of your car. Will you answer my question, please?"

"Of course not. I put it in my pocket. I'm certain...." Julia stopped. Could it possibly have slipped out of her pocket? Although she doubted that had happened, it wasn't impossible. What if she was wrong about Prescott?

"Mr. Prescott came to the station, and we talked for quite a while about your past relationship with him."

Julia raised her eyebrows. "My *relationship* with him? I have no relationship with that man. He's a criminal I helped send to prison." She stared at the officer through narrowed eyes. "Just what did he tell you?"

Officer Frett flushed. "He told me that his case was overturned. He seems to think you're upset about the way things turned out and wonders if that might have influenced your suspicion that he was behind the theft."

"Excuse me?"

"Look, Mrs. Foley. You seem like a nice lady, but you have a history with this man. It seems he's already been accused of a crime he didn't commit. Now it appears to be happening again. You can surely understand his feeling of being somewhat...persecuted."

Julia was so shocked she couldn't respond. Grady Prescott was trying to claim that she was persecuting him?

She stood up. "Officer Frett, I realize you're simply trying to do your job the best way you can. I have nothing against you. But Grady Prescott is a thief and a con man. I think he took my wallet, and I also believe he's guilty of the crimes in Atlanta. I can't expect you to understand this based on the information you have at this time, but I would like to ask that you keep an open mind. Even if he hadn't committed those particular crimes in Atlanta, he had a long record before those incidents."

Officer Frett stood up too. "I'll keep an open mind, Mrs. Foley, but I have to ask you to do the same and not harass Mr. Prescott. He's considering filing a restraining order against you."

When she was a kid, Julia had watched cartoons with characters that got so upset the tops of their heads blew off. If this were a cartoon, Julia was certain that's what would be happening to her. But this was real life, and she knew she had to restrain herself.

"Thank you for coming to see me, Officer Frett. I hope you will keep an eye on Grady Prescott, because he is certainly up to something. I think it's tied to the theft that occurred at Hudson's Rare Coins the night of the grits contest. I'm asking you to consider that possibility. And as far as Mr. Prescott is concerned, you can tell him that I have no intention of going anywhere near him. He is the one who has approached me on two different occasions. Once when he purposely ran into me at the grits contest and again, when he came to my office. I have never tried to contact him. Not once. So perhaps you should tell him that restraining orders go both ways."

"That's very true," Officer Frett said. "I hope I haven't upset you. I came here because I felt you needed to know we caught the man who had your wallet. I'm glad it was returned to you. We are holding Mr. Randolph for the theft." He turned to walk out of her office, but Julia called him back.

"I'm sorry to bother you, but we understand you have some film from Lyndon Perry. He works for Channel 6."

"Yes, we do."

"I want to explain…."

Officer Frett put up his hand. "We spoke to Mrs. Sims. She told us what happened. We're satisfied with her explanation."

Well, at least that was a relief. "Thank you, Officer."

"You're welcome." He left, and Julia stared after him. If she had dropped her wallet it would have been easy prey for a thief. She had no reason not to believe that it had ended up in Cliff Randolph's possession. But what she couldn't accept was that the same day her wallet disappeared, Grady Prescott showed up and just happened to run into her. Julia trusted her instincts, and a voice inside her was telling her that Prescott was up to something—and for some reason he'd decided to drag her into it.

Chapter Twenty-One

A FEW MINUTES AFTER OFFICER Frett left, Meredith came into Julia's office. "What was he doing here?" she asked Julia.

Julia leaned forward and put her head in her hands. "You won't believe it. They arrested someone for stealing my wallet. And before you ask, it wasn't Grady Prescott. It's some other guy. Probably the man who found the wallet after Prescott dumped it. I think he purposely threw it out in the parking lot near your car hoping someone would take it. Now the police think I'm trying to accuse him unjustly...just like I did in Atlanta."

"You're kidding." Meredith sat down in the chair the officer had just vacated. "So Prescott was counting on someone picking up your wallet and trying to use your cards?"

Julia shrugged. "Well, I guess he figured that if it was found and returned, he would still be in the clear. But if it was stolen and I blamed him..."

"He looks like a victim," Meredith finished. She was quiet for a moment before saying, "Is there any chance you could have accidentally dropped it?"

"Oh, Meredith. Not you too." Julia sighed. "I'm sorry, but that's just too much of a coincidence for me. I know in my gut Prescott is behind the theft of my wallet."

"Okay."

Julia lifted an eyebrow. "Okay? Don't you want to ask me if I'm prejudiced against Grady Prescott because his conviction was over-turned? I mean, I could have made a mistake in Atlanta, and now I'm making another one. Don't you want to grill me…even a little?"

"No."

Julia stared at her for a moment. "Why not?"

Meredith sighed. "Look, Julia, if you're sure Prescott is involved, that's all I need to know. I trust your instincts." She leaned forward in her chair. "I have no idea why he took your wallet. It doesn't make sense. We'll find the truth as long as we don't dismiss all these events as coincidence. As Sherlock Holmes said, 'Life is infinitely stranger than anything which the mind of man could invent.' All these inci-dents may look like coincidence, but if you don't think they are, I believe you."

Julia smiled at her. "Have I ever told you how much I appreciate you?"

"Yeah. A few times."

"Well, add one more."

Meredith laughed. "So what do we do next?"

"Before I answer that, I do have some good news, believe it or not. The police saw Lyndon's film and aren't worried that Maribelle was involved in what happened. At least we don't need to worry about that."

"That's wonderful. I would hate to see her dragged into this any more than she already has been."

"Me too. And as far as what we do next? I'm not sure. We still have two people to talk to. Martin Seeger from the Seaside Grill and Cyrus Sharrah from Sharrah's on River Street."

"Let's hope we get more from them than what we have from the others so far," Meredith said. "We still need to figure out how the paprika that Jerome tasted was just paprika and a short time later it was ground ghost peppers. We know it was okay when he picked the jar up. If it had contained ghost pepper, he would have reacted violently when he tasted it."

"That really confuses me," Julia said slowly. "The contents of the jar changed sometime between when it left the coffee shop with Jerome and when the contestants added it to their grits. How can that be?"

"Are you thinking that the paprika was dumped out and the ghost pepper was added?"

"But there's a problem with that theory," Julia said. "Handling ghost peppers, even those that are ground, isn't easy. Remember when I checked out the bottle at the contest? Just touching it burned my fingers."

"Okay," Meredith said. "But the contestants were wearing food handlers' gloves. Wouldn't that have protected them?"

Julia nodded. "You're right, but it would still be really difficult to switch the contents with people watching."

"So you think someone switched jars?"

"That's the more likely explanation. The substitution would have been easy. Two bottles that look the same. Take the paprika and substitute a jar that looked exactly the same with the ghost pepper."

"Of course," Meredith said. "I certainly wish we had more video from the contest. By the time Lyndon began filming, the substitution had already occurred."

"There were three local news stations there that night," Julia said. "Maybe someone else has some earlier footage."

"It's not impossible," Meredith said. "I'll call around and see if anyone else had their cameras going before Lyndon began filming. And you know, the way everyone takes pictures and videos with their phones now, others at the contest could have filmed something or taken photos that will show us more than we know now. But how do we find those people?"

"Well, we call the TV stations first. We could place an ad in the paper, but I'd hate for a reporter to see it and start something that would embarrass Charlene."

Meredith was quiet for a moment. "What if we just asked for video and pictures from the contest that night and didn't say who we were?"

"When they call us, they'd be able to figure it out pretty quickly."

"Yeah, you're right." Meredith sighed. "I guess we'll need to do some old-fashioned investigative work. Just like Sherlock Holmes."

Julia grinned. "Well, if it was good enough for him…"

Meredith laughed. "Ron knew Martin Seeger. He did some work for him once. Let me see if he'll meet with us."

"This is the second time we've been able to connect with someone because of Ron. It makes it feel as if he's helping us, making certain we get the information we need."

"Yes, it does," Meredith said softly. "That thought has crossed my mind more than once since I took over the agency."

"I know he'd be proud of you, Mere. Magnolia Investigations is succeeding because of you."

"Because of both of us," she said with a smile. "I couldn't possibly have kept things going without you."

"You're going to make me cry."

"Let's get back to business before we both get too emotional."

"Deal."

"So what about Sharrah's on River Street?"

"It's a great restaurant," Julia said. "Pricy and rather ostentatious, but the food is worth it. Beau likes it."

"Yeah, Ron did too. Why don't we all have dinner there Friday night?"

"I'm sure Beau would love to go," Julia said. "What about Quin?"

"I'll ask him."

"Tell him it's a business thing. We need him for cover."

Meredith chortled. "For cover? We sound like spies."

Julia shrugged. "Well, in this situation, we are, right?"

"I guess. I'll ask him. I'll also call Martin to see if we can drop by the Seaside Grill and talk to him."

"Okay," Julia said. "And I'll see if I can get us reservations Friday night at Sharrah's."

Meredith got up and left the office. After calling Sharrah's, Julia tried to take care of some paperwork that needed her attention, but her mind kept drifting back to her conversation with Officer Frett. Regardless of what she felt her gut was telling her, his comments had shaken her. Were they going in the wrong direction? Was she so concentrated on Grady Prescott that she was seeing everything colored by his sudden appearance in Savannah? She prayed it wasn't true and that God would help her to see this case clearly.

Chapter Twenty-Two

A LITTLE AFTER TWO IN the afternoon, Julia and Meredith arrived at the Seaside Grill. Meredith's calls to the other television stations yielded nothing. None of them had anything different than what they'd already seen. Julia was beginning to wonder when they would get a break.

When they entered the restaurant, they were greeted by a hostess who seemed to know they were coming. She directed them to a table in the corner and asked them to wait. After thanking her for her help, Julia and Meredith sat down. Julia glanced around the room. Even this late in the day, the restaurant was still busy. Decorated with a nod to the restaurant's name, large nets hung from the ceiling and the walls were decorated with paintings of various sea creatures. Light blues were blended with white and darker blues to create a beachy feeling. The decorator had obviously gone for a seaside motif with a relaxed ambience. Julia felt it had been achieved. The dining room was light and airy and created the expectation that any moment diners would hear the calming sounds of waves washing up against the shore.

They'd just sat down when a waiter came to their table. Although they'd had lunch, Julia didn't want to offend Martin. She ordered a shrimp cocktail and an iced tea. One of the things the Seaside Grill was known for was its freshly brewed tea. Meredith followed Julia's lead and ordered the same thing.

When the waiter walked away, Meredith said quietly, "That shrimp cocktail is as expensive as an entire meal at Peachie's."

Julia smiled. "I know, but I don't want to sit here without ordering something. Makes us look like we're only here to interrogate Martin."

Meredith sighed before saying, "But we are."

"I realize that, but I don't want Martin to know it. I really hope he can help us."

"Well, no matter what, this will be a treat. I love shrimp cocktail but rarely order it."

Julia noticed Martin coming out of the kitchen and speaking to their waitress. She pointed at them. Meredith smiled and lifted her hand so he would see them. He said something else to the waitress and then headed their way.

"Hello, ladies," he said when he reached them. He held his hand out to Meredith. "So nice to see you again. How are you doing?"

"I'm doing well," she said. "I kept Ron's business open and am running it with my friend." She nodded toward Julia. "This is Julia Foley, the other half of Magnolia Investigations."

Martin reached out and shook Julia's hand as well. He had a strong, firm grip. He was a nice-looking man with dark curly hair and dark eyes. He exuded self-confidence. He sat down and smiled at Meredith, his teeth sparkling white against his dark skin. "So what can I do for you?" he asked.

"Martin, you probably read the article in the paper about the grits contest?"

"Yes, I did. In my opinion it was very unfair. Made it sound as if the Downhome Diner was somehow responsible."

"I agree," Meredith said. "Charlene hired us to find out what really happened. To be honest with you, so far we're not having much luck. We've talked to quite a few people, but we still can't figure out how that jar of pepper got on the table."

Martin frowned. "Cyrus Sharrah told me that Jerome Matheson from Mama Louise's kitchen put it there. When I asked Cyrus why, he told me that one of the judges was partial to paprika on grits and that the TV people needed additional color added to the finished dishes so they would look appetizing to the television audience."

"Did he mention which judge?"

Martin nodded. "Ernie Prothro."

"Did you find that unusual?" Julia asked.

"Absolutely. I mean, paprika is used frequently in grits, don't get me wrong, but judges should be critiquing entries based on how the chef prepares the food. Not a judge's own preferences. Especially something that has little or nothing to do with the taste."

"Maribelle Sims from the Downhome Diner said you told her it was there in case anyone wanted to use it, but you didn't say anything to her about Ernie or the television aspect."

"That's true. At the time I wasn't certain the message was one that should be shared."

Although Martin seemed sincere, Julia wasn't so sure. He'd used the supposed paprika. If he was so against the idea of Ernie trying to manipulate the contestants, why would he go ahead and sprinkle it on his food?

"Can I ask why you decided to use the paprika?"

He sighed. "Normally, I wouldn't have, but after the others used it, I decided I didn't want to lose the contest because of something so petty."

"Did you notice anything else, Martin?" Meredith asked. "Anything that seemed unusual, besides the paprika?"

He was quiet as he appeared to consider Meredith's question. Finally he shook his head. "I don't think so, but I'll try to go over it in my mind later. Right now I'm just too busy." He started to get up but then stopped and sat back down. "There is one thing. What kind of pepper was in the jar?"

"It was ground ghost peppers," Julia said.

Martin nodded. "I suspected that." He sighed. "I should have tasted it before putting it on my grits. I keep asking myself why I didn't. It only occurred to me later that it could have been placed there by another contestant who thought they could win the contest by getting some of us to ruin our dishes."

"Why didn't you consider that possibility at the time?" Julia asked.

He paused for a moment. "I think it was because of Ernie Prothro. His name holds a lot of influence in this town. It would never occur to me that he might be up to anything unethical." Martin shrugged. "And then of course we were all so focused on the contest. I guess I just didn't think it through the way I should have."

"Thank you for talking to us about this, Martin," Meredith said. "We really appreciate it."

"The Downhome Diner is awesome. Love the food and the history. I'm certain they had nothing to do with what happened. If I can do anything to help, please let me know."

"I appreciate that. We will."

Martin frowned. "Have you ordered?"

"Yes. Your incredible shrimp cocktail for both of us."

"No, no, no," he said, grinning. "You don't get out of here without dessert. How about the best bread pudding you've ever tasted?"

Before they had a chance to respond, their waiter came up to the table with their iced teas and shrimp cocktails on a tray.

"Roberto," Martin said to him, "after they finish their cocktails, bring them each a piece of bread pudding. Everything's on me."

"Yes sir," Roberto said with a wide smile.

"Good to see you, Meredith," Martin said. "And nice to meet you, Julia. I hope you'll both come back when you can. And I'll call you if I think of anything that might help, Meredith." With that, he hurried off.

"You'll love the bread pudding," Roberto said. "It's topped with a brown sugar butter sauce. Truly decadent."

"I wonder," Julia said. "Could you remove the calories for us?"

Roberto laughed. "No, but when you eat this bread pudding you'll realize the calories don't count."

"That's good to know," Julia said with a smile.

"Can I get you anything else right now?" Roberto asked.

"No, thank you," Meredith said.

As Roberto walked away, Julia sighed. "This may be the first case we've ever had that should come with its own diet."

"I hear you," Meredith said with a laugh. "At least the shrimp cocktail isn't fattening."

"Yeah. That's nice until bread pudding covered with brown sugar butter sauce knocks our allotted caloric intake into next week." Julia speared one of the giant shrimp hanging over the side of the chilled cut-glass goblet and dipped it into the red sauce sitting in a small bowl next to it. The shrimp was cold and delicious, and the sauce had just the right amount of tangy goodness.

"This is awesome," Meredith said after eating her first shrimp.

"I have a feeling it will be hard going back to bologna sandwiches after this," Julia grumbled.

Meredith giggled. "Julia Foley, you don't eat bologna sandwiches."

"No, but whatever I do have for lunch will probably taste like a bologna sandwich in comparison to all this great food."

"Good point. Have you ever made bread pudding?" Meredith asked.

"Yes, years ago. Not sure why I stopped. I guess I started concentrating more on the kinds of things Beau likes. Not that he didn't like my bread pudding. He just loves—"

"Anything with chocolate?"

Julia smiled. "Yes." She put her fork down and stared at Meredith. "So what do you think about what Martin said?"

"Well, it coincides completely with the accounts from Maribelle and Jerome. I think they're all telling us the truth."

"I do too. Unfortunately, that doesn't help us." She frowned. "Somewhere between the time that Jerome picked up the note and the paprika and the contestants added it to their dishes, it changed from something mild and unthreatening to ground ghost peppers. But no one noticed anything. Nothing was caught on video that we know of. So who changed it? And when?"

"Personally, I think it could have been almost anyone. People were scrambling around, trying to get ready for the contest and the television cameras. Someone could have ridden a camel down the street, right in front of them, and they wouldn't have noticed."

Julia raised an eyebrow. "A camel? Really?"

Meredith laughed. "Okay, they probably would have noticed. How about one of those cute little pygmy goats?"

It was Julia's turn to laugh. "I'll give you that." She sighed. "So I guess we're left with Cyrus Sharrah. If he can't help us, I think we're stuck."

"You're forgetting the coin shop. Why don't we go by there this afternoon and talk to them?"

Julia nodded. "I'm not sure they have any information that will help us, but I still wonder if the situation at the contest was created for a diversion so the thieves would have more time to get away."

"It's possible," Meredith said. "The coin shop won't have information about our ghost pepper problem, but I'll feel better knowing we talked to everyone involved and did all we could to find out what actually happened."

"We'll just have to keep digging," Julia said. "Someone put that ghost pepper in the paprika bottle, and I want to know why."

Chapter Twenty-Three

IT WAS ALMOST FOUR O'CLOCK by the time they got to the coin shop. It was in a strip mall, surrounded by stores with high-end clothing, a nice restaurant, a pet store, and a jewelry store.

As they parked, Meredith nudged Julia. "I've been in that jewelry store. Very nice. They have some rather expensive pieces. So why rob a coin shop instead of this place?"

"I don't know," Julia said slowly. Meredith had made a good point. "Let's go there first. We won't stay long. I want to ask them a couple of questions."

Meredith nodded. "The coin shop closes at six. We have time."

They got out of the car and went inside the jewelry store. Julia checked out a couple of the display cases. Meredith was right. Some very nice pieces. Some of them extremely expensive. So why rob the coin shop when this place would have been a more lucrative target?

An older woman approached them. "May I help you ladies?" she asked.

"I'm Meredith Bellefontaine, and this is my partner, Julia Foley," Meredith said. "We're investigators, and we'd like to ask you a few questions."

"Certainly. I'm Ann Marschand, the manager. What do you want to know?"

"Friday night there was a grits contest on River Street. Did you hear about it?"

Ann nodded. "My daughter and her friend were there. Unfortunately, it was called off."

"Do you know why?" Julia asked.

"We were told that the contestants mistook a jar of hot pepper for paprika and sprinkled it on their grits." Ann smiled. "I'm certain the people involved were not amused, but it is rather humorous."

"Yes, it really is, but our friend has been accused of trying to sabotage the contest," Meredith said. "We're trying to prove it isn't true."

Ann raised her eyebrows. "I'm sorry to hear that. But what does that have to do with us?"

Julia cleared her throat. A couple was looking at wedding rings with another clerk, and she didn't want them to overhear her. "We're getting ready to talk to the people in the coin shop that was robbed. We think the two incidents might be connected. But when we pulled into the parking lot, we noticed your store. It seems to us that you would have been a better target than the coin shop."

"We thought it was odd too," Ann said, her voice soft. "We have a safe for our most expensive items. But we were still here when the robbery in the coin shop occurred, so our safe was open. They could have forced their way in and made off with quite a bit of valuable jewelry. Of course we have an excellent security system. If anyone had tried to enter after the door was locked, the police would have been automatically contacted."

"I would assume the coin shop has a similar security system."

Ann nodded. "Actually, they work with the same security company we do. I have no idea if we have the same plan."

"We heard the shop had a very expensive coin and that it was taken," Meredith said.

Ann looked around before saying, "If they did, it's extremely unusual. Most of their inventory consisted of coins worth no more than a few hundred dollars. In my opinion, if a coin like the one reported stolen was in their possession, the thieves must have known they had it. It's the only reason they'd be robbed now."

"It looks like they close at the same time you do," Julia said. "Six?"

"Yes. But we're still here for another thirty minutes, straightening up, putting items in the safe. I think the coin shop has a similar pattern. Most nights we leave about the same time."

"Do you know any of the employees?" Meredith asked.

"Not really. Dale Henshaw owns the store. We've had a few conversations, and he's been here a couple of times to buy jewelry for his wife. Christmas and anniversary presents."

"Any of the other employees come in to make a purchase?"

Julia was wondering why Meredith was so interested in who Ann knew from the coin shop.

"Well, yes. Yesterday one of them was here to purchase a very expensive ring."

"What kind of ring?" Julia asked.

"An engagement ring. I asked her where her fiancé was. She said he was out of the country and told her to pick out any ring she wanted." Ann shrugged. "It happens, but it's rare. Usually, couples come in here together."

"Can I ask the price of the ring she bought?" Meredith asked.

Ann looked around again then lowered her voice. "I can't tell you that, but let's just say I could feed my family for a year with what she spent on that ring."

"Wow," Julia said. "Her fiancé must be loaded."

Ann nodded. "That's what I thought. She paid for the ring, but it's still here, being sized."

"When is she supposed to pick it up?" Meredith asked.

"Tomorrow."

"Ann," Meredith said, "is there any way you can stall her a little? I have to wonder if she was involved in the robbery. Someone obviously had inside information. Knew that an expensive coin would be in the shop. Then after the robbery, an employee comes here and buys an extremely expensive ring? That a little too coincidental to me."

Ann seemed to study Meredith for a moment. "I think I can stall her, but not for long. I'll need to release the ring as soon as possible. I hate to withhold a purchase from one of our customers."

"All right," Meredith said. "We'll do what we can. But if I'm right, that ring could end up as evidence."

"I understand." At that moment, the door opened and two people walked in. Ann looked at them and smiled. Then she turned back to Meredith and Julia. "I've got to go," she whispered. "A couple of our best customers just walked in."

"All right. Thank you," Meredith said. "And if anything odd happens and you need to reach us, here's our number." She reached into her purse and pulled out her card. "My cell phone number is on here and so is our office number. Call anytime."

"Thank you," Ann said. "I'm glad someone's looking into that situation. I've been wondering about it."

"We'll do our best to find the truth, Ann," Julia said. "Thank you for talking to us."

"You're welcome."

As Ann walked toward the couple that was waiting near the entrance, Julia looked at Meredith and said in hushed tones, "You think someone in the coin shop helped to coordinate the robbery?"

"Shh," she said. "Let's go outside."

Julia left the jewelry store, Meredith behind her. Once they were on the sidewalk, Meredith said, "How did the robbers know about that coin? Sounds as if they don't normally handle that kind of merchandise. And then one of the employees buys an expensive piece of jewelry? Don't you find that odd?"

"You think her fiancé gave her part of the proceeds? If we find him, we find the thief?"

Meredith sighed. "I hope so." She shrugged. "Let's talk to the people at the coin shop. Of course, even if we think we can prove some kind of collusion, we still have to convince the police to take a look at it."

Julia nodded. "You're right."

They walked down the sidewalk until they reached the coin shop. The large store window read HUDSON'S RARE COINS. When they opened the door, they stepped into a shop that looked very much like the jewelry store. Glass display cases lined the walls with two others in the middle. Julia was impressed.

A man who was standing behind one of the counters saw them and walked around the display case. "Can I help you?" he asked.

"We're investigating the robbery that occurred here Friday night," Meredith said. "Can I ask you some questions?"

The man looked confused. "We already talked to the police," he said.

Julia read his name tag. DALE HENSHAW. The owner. As Meredith explained who they were and why they were there, Julia studied the other employees. A man, probably in his early thirties, and a young woman. The woman had long chestnut brown hair that flowed over her shoulders, reminding Julia of a spilled cup of hot chocolate. Her large dark eyes were focused on them, not on the coins she had in front of her. Julia could see that she was nervous. Could this be the woman Ann had told them about? While Meredith talked to Mr. Henshaw, Julia decided to have a conversation with her.

Julia walked up to the case the woman stood behind. "So do you just work here or are you also a collector?" she asked.

The woman shrugged. "I'm trying to start a collection, but I just have some inexpensive coins so far. Dale…Mr. Henshaw got me interested in them."

"Coins are fascinating. What about your husband? Does he collect coins?"

"I'm not married," she said. "I just got engaged."

Julia looked at her name tag. CRYSTAL. "Congratulations." She looked at Crystal's ring finger.

Crystal must have read her thoughts, because she smiled. "My engagement ring is over at the jewelry store being sized. It's beautiful. My fiancé spent a lot of money on it."

"So you two went and picked it out together?"

"No, he's in the army reserve. He was called overseas for a while. He gave me a check before he left and told me I could pick out my own ring." This time her smile widened. "It cost over ten thousand dollars. I just love it."

The owner cleared his throat, and Crystal switched to all business. "Is there something I can show you?" she asked.

"Oh, no thank you. My partner and I are investigating an incident that occurred Friday night. Well, actually two events. Something that happened during a food competition on River Street and the theft of a rare coin from your shop. We think they might be related."

The color drained from the woman's face. It was obvious the investigators were on the right track. She was absolutely terrified.

Chapter Twenty-Four

JULIA WATCHED AS CRYSTAL TRIED to recover. She cleared her throat and said, "I'm sorry. I don't know anything about that. You'll need to talk to our owner, Mr. Henshaw."

She turned away from Julia and disappeared through a door in the back of the large room. It was clear the question had rattled her. Julia was certain that even if Crystal wasn't directly involved, she certainly had information about the theft.

Julia walked over to where Meredith was still talking to the owner. "Mr. Henshaw, this is my partner, Julia Foley," Meredith said.

"Nice to meet you," Julia said.

Henshaw nodded. "You too. I was telling Mrs. Bellefontaine that we were surprised by the theft on Friday. We were very careful to keep news of the coin quiet so it would be protected. No one knew about it except us and the man who intended to buy it. I've worked with him for years and know him to be above suspicion."

"Did you give the police the buyer's name?" Meredith asked.

"Yes, I did. I'm sure they've spoken to him by now. He was very upset about losing the chance to own the coin."

"I understand it was extremely rare," Julia said.

"Yes. It's a type one 1853 O Seated Liberty Half Dollar. There are no arrowheads at the date and no rays on the reverse." Henshaw sighed in obvious awe of the coin. "There were only four of these coins known to exist. This would have been the fifth."

"Why are there are only five of them?" Meredith asked.

"The New Orleans Mint only produced a few of them in 1853 before the new dies with the arrows and rays included arrived from the Philadelphia Mint Headquarters."

"Do you have any idea how news of the coin got out?" Julia asked. She had to force herself not to look back to see if Crystal had returned.

"None. Donnie and Crystal have been with me a long time. I trust them both completely, and none of us breathed a word." He shook his head. "We were to meet with the buyer Saturday morning. I hated calling him to tell him the coin was gone."

"How did you acquire it?" Meredith asked.

"Someone came to us, wanting to sell. A woman here in Savannah who found it in her grandfather's possessions after he died. She'd looked it up and knew it was valuable. We settled on a price, and I purchased it. I was able to contact a couple of coin buyers I knew would be interested and accepted a bid from one of them. We would have made a tidy sum on it."

"Was it insured?" Julia asked.

"Oh yes. I'm very careful to make certain our most valuable pieces are." He shrugged. "We'll get back the money we spent on it as well as what we would have made from the buyer. This won't hurt us financially at all. However, it won't help our reputation. It may take a while to prove to people that they can trust us with their coins, but eventually we'll recover. I'm not very worried about that.

The real damage caused by the loss of such a valuable coin is… Well, to those of us who love coins, it's devastating."

"Won't it be almost impossible for the thieves to sell the coin?" Meredith asked. "I assume the word goes out quickly to coin dealers across the country that the coin was stolen."

"You're right. Unfortunately, there is a black market for rare coins. Someone will buy it and keep it for several years. Then someone will suddenly *find it*. At that point, unless there is something wrong with their story that makes the authorities suspicious, they'll be able to sell it. You see, no one is certain how many of these coins are out there. There could be others. And there's no way to prove a particular coin was stolen. We can't mark it in any way. And this one, which was in fine condition, had no odd scratches or defects that would make it easy to identify."

"Can you tell us exactly what happened Friday night?" Meredith asked.

Henshaw pursed his lips. "It was just a few minutes before closing. The door opened, and two men came in. One of them had a ski mask on, and the other was putting his on as he entered. He had his back to us, so we couldn't see his face."

"Then what happened?" Meredith asked.

"The first man pulled out a gun while the second one flipped our sign to CLOSED. He turned the lock on the door and pulled down the shades on the windows."

"What about your security system?"

"He knew about it. Ordered us not to turn it on or he would shoot one of us. Then he grabbed Crystal and told me he wanted the coin. He knew exactly what it was. He said he wanted the 1853 O Seated Liberty Half Dollar, and if I didn't get it immediately, Crystal would die." Henshaw's eyes grew shiny. "Of course I got the coin. It was important to me, but it wasn't worth the life of one of my employees."

"Did he look at any other coins?" Julia asked.

Henshaw shook his head. "No, he knew just what he wanted. Once I gave him the coin, he ordered us to sit down on the floor. He tied our hands with plastic ties and told us we were not to contact the police for one hour or he would come back and hurt our families."

Julia and Meredith looked at each other. "So did you wait?"

"No. I wanted to, but Donnie was able to get his hands free. He called the police right away. I would have waited, but Donnie said the robbers were going to be too busy getting away. They had no intention of coming near us or our families, because the police would be watching us. He was right. The police have been wonderful about keeping an eye on us even though they don't think we're really in any danger."

Donnie came over to where they stood talking to Henshaw. He was a nice-looking young man who seemed very concerned about his employer. "I'm sorry to interrupt, but one of the men said something odd. The police didn't seem interested, but it still bothers me."

"And what was that?" Meredith asked.

Donnie frowned. "He said something about finding gravy. It was weird."

"Gravy? Are you sure?" Julia asked. "Could you have misheard? Could he have said *Grady*?"

"I...I don't know. I was certain he said gravy. He mumbled something I couldn't hear, and then he said they had to hurry up and find gravy."

Julia looked at Meredith. "You say you told the police this and they weren't interested."

Donnie nodded. "They looked at me like I was crazy."

Was this the proof they'd been looking for? Could this finally tie Grady Prescott to the robbery?

Chapter Twenty-Five

Julia's first reaction was one of excitement. If they could prove Prescott was involved in the robbery…

"Thanks, Donnie," Meredith said. She took Julia's arm and led her a few feet away. "You can't tell the police that the man was actually saying *Grady*."

"Why not?" Julia asked. Before Meredith had a chance to respond, Julia answered her own question. "Because Prescott has me looking like some kind of unhinged woman trying to harass him since his sentence was overturned." She shook her head. "That's what this is all about, Meredith. He knew I was in Savannah and set me up as someone he could use to get the police off his trail. They won't believe a word I say. They don't want me anywhere near him. I'll bet he planned this even before the robbery. Bump into me. Take my wallet. Make it look like I'm stalking him. That way anything I say makes me look bad and takes the attention off him." She looked into Meredith's eyes. "He played this perfectly. Take the one person who could convince the police to take a closer look at him, and make her look unhinged. Go one step further and use her as his alibi."

"Well, maybe."

Julia was surprised by Meredith's comment. "Surely you see this too?"

"I'm not sure. From what you've told me, he doesn't seem like someone capable of planning something this elaborate. And how would he know ahead of time that you'd be at the grits contest?"

Meredith had a point. Prescott wasn't an organized thief. This did seem a little too sophisticated for him.

"Let's talk about this a little later, okay?" Meredith suggested.

Julia nodded and then looked around the shop. Crystal was nowhere to be seen. "Mr. Henshaw, please don't be offended by this question, but how can you be so sure one of your employees didn't say something that alerted the thieves that a valuable coin was in your shop?"

Henshaw looked surprised by the question. "I…well, like I told the police, we're a family. I'd trust these two with my life."

"I know you hear people say things like that all the time," Donnie said, "but we really are a family. I was in a lot of trouble when I was younger. Spent some time in jail. But Mr. Henshaw gave me a chance. Changed my life. I would sooner die than betray him. And I know Crystal feels the same way."

His gaze swung around the store, but Julia had noticed Crystal still hadn't returned. Donnie frowned but didn't seem too concerned.

Julia took a deep breath. "So you're not worried about Crystal's expensive new ring?"

A look crossed Henshaw's face that almost made Julia regret she'd asked the question.

"No, of course not," he said slowly. It seemed the idea that the robbery and the ring might be connected hadn't occurred to him before.

"You're wrong if you think Crystal was involved in this," Donnie said sharply. "She loves Dale just as much as I do. She was homeless for a while after her mother kicked her out. Dale met her at church, just like me. He helped her get her life together. There's no way she'd steal from him."

"Church?" Meredith asked.

"I belong to the Savannah First Assembly of God," Henshaw said. "We have an outreach to kids in trouble. We provide food, shelter, and education to young people who are homeless or who have been in jail. We've had a lot of success. Donnie and Crystal are two of our champions. They both have good jobs, their own apartments, and are upstanding citizens. I'm proud of both of them." This time he stared at the back door.

"What does that door lead to?" Meredith asked.

"Storage room and bathroom," Henshaw said. "There's also a door that opens up to the alley. We only use it when we take the trash out to the dumpster."

Julia could hear the worried tone in his voice.

"I'll check on her," Donnie said.

As he headed toward the back room, Henshaw frowned at Meredith and Julia. "Surely you don't think Crystal had anything to do with this theft?"

Julia's heart hurt for the man. He was obviously a very trusting person who couldn't accept that someone he'd helped could turn on him.

"We don't know," she said. "We're just checking out the possibilities. One of the contestants suggested publicly that our friends caused the problems at the grits competition. It hurt their reputation, and we're trying to clear their names." She shook her head. "Look, we're not accusing Crystal of anything. As you said, it probably had nothing to do with her." Even as she said the words, her gut told her it was Crystal. She'd probably given the information to her boyfriend, who'd robbed the shop. But was Prescott involved? She suspected it, but they would need more evidence to prove something.

Donnie came back into the room. "She's gone, Dale. Took her purse, and her car isn't here."

Henshaw turned gray and swayed. Julia came around the side of the display case and took his arm. "Please Mr. Henshaw, sit down. Everything will be all right."

Donnie pulled one of the stools sitting behind the counter over to Henshaw, who collapsed onto it. "She's like a daughter to me," he said. "Or at least that's what I thought."

"Sometimes people do things without thinking about the consequences," Julia said. "Did Crystal know about the insurance?"

"We both did," Donnie said.

"Maybe she thought taking the coin wouldn't hurt you," Julia said gently. "Sometimes we're able to convince ourselves of things when we have to. My guess is that's what happened here."

"You need to call the police," Meredith said.

"I don't want to get her into trouble."

"Mr. Henshaw…," Julia began.

"Dale. Please. Just call me Dale."

"All right, Dale. Finding her now will keep her out of even more trouble. Besides, if the police bring her in early, she may be able to make a deal. Turn over the actual thieves and stay out of prison."

"Really?"

"Yes. So far all we suspect her of is telling someone else about the coin. If the police can locate her before the coin is sold, she may be able to stay out of more serious trouble."

"All right. I'll call them now," he said. "Who should I ask for?"

"Try Officer Frett," Julia said. "He knows about the case. I can't promise that he'll have the authority to make a deal for Crystal though. You'll need to ask him about that." She turned to Meredith. "Crystal said her boyfriend is in the army reserve. That he was called overseas for a while."

Meredith shook her head slowly. "Army reservists hardly ever go out of the country. They serve in the states, usually in positions temporarily vacated by army personnel who are called overseas."

"So her boyfriend lied to her?" Julia asked.

"I'm certain he did."

Dale got up from his stool and walked over to the front door, where he turned the OPEN sign over to CLOSED. "Let's call the police," he said.

Chapter Twenty-Six

May 1895

"Maddie Louise Greer, you get in here right now, young lady."

When Bessie's daughter came into the kitchen, it was obvious she wanted to be with her brother. They'd been play-ing with the toys their father had made for for them: a large wooden house with many rooms and carved figures that included women, men, children, and animals. Justice had a talent with wood. When he wasn't tending to their farm, he liked to carve. He'd sold many items to their neighbors and friends. She was so proud of him. He was a good man. Her mother would have approved if she'd just lived long enough. She died of influenza not long before Bessie met Justice. Bessie missed her every day.

"What do you want, Mama?" Maddie asked impatiently.

"First of all, don't sass me, girl. When I call, you come runnin'. You understand?"

"Yes'm," Maddie said. Her expression, however, made it clear she wasn't happy.

"You're twelve years old. I know you're still a child, but you're gonna be a woman soon. You'll be gettin' married. I want you to learn how to cook." Bessie sighed. "Every time I try to teach you, your mind wanders off somewhere else. I don't know if you're hearin' me or not."

Maddie marched over to the kitchen table and pulled out a chair. When she sat down she frowned at her mother. "What if I don't want to get married, Mama? What if I want to be something else? Like a lawyer...or a doctor."

Bessie stared at her daughter. What could she tell her? "Maddie, you know there aren't any Black lawyers or doctors in Savannah. It's a wonderful goal, but—"

"Mama, Macon Allen is a lawyer. And Alice McKane is talking about opening a school for Black nurses in Savannah."

"I know about Macon Allen. He can barely support himself. People don't want a Black attorney. And talkin' about opening a school...is just talk." She smiled at her daughter. "I'm grateful that you want to do something special with your life. You're so smart and creative. But there still aren't many opportunities for Black people. Someday maybe..."

"I don't want to wait on someday," Maddie said. Her jaw jutted out, a sign that she had made up her mind and nothing could make her change it.

"I swear, girl. You are so stubborn."

"I take after my mother."

Bessie couldn't help but laugh. "All right. And I love that you're a fighter. But..." She wiped away unbidden tears that suddenly filled her eyes.

"Mama, I didn't mean to make you cry," Maddie said. Her expression changed from obstinate determination to concern for her mother.

"You didn't make me cry," Bessie said, wiping her face with her apron. "I just wish you'd known your grandmother. That woman was the strongest person I ever knew, but even she wouldn't have thought about bein' a doctor or a lawyer. There were no opportunities for things like that when she was alive. Yet she made sure me and your uncle Joseph went to school. She wanted us to be educated so we could do something special in life."

"But Mama, you're just a teacher. You don't do anything special."

Bessie tried to ignore the hurt her daughter's words caused. She had half a mind to send Maddie to her room for being so disrespectful. But she took a deep breath instead and decided her child needed to understand what was truly important in life. "Yes, I'm a teacher and, even more important, I'm a wife and mother. I think that's very special, Maddie. Maybe my generation won't be the one that will break all the barriers for Black people, but yours might be. And if not you, then maybe your children." She reached over and took her daughter's hand. "Being special isn't determined by what you do, Maddie. Being special is determined by who you are inside, and who is inside you. God has been helping this family for many years. My mama and daddy were freed long before many others. And then Mother Mathilda came along and educated me. Now you're in school, learning even more than I did. You see, God has a special plan for all of us. But I believe we need to put our hands to whatever He puts in front of us now. If we do that, we'll be on the exact path He has for us. And that will lead us into doing very, very special things. Do you understand? You need to quit worryin' so much about the future. Cast your care on the Lord, Maddie. He won't ignore those yearnings in your heart. Trust Him."

For the first time since she'd entered the kitchen, Maddie smiled. Bessie really was proud of her...and her brother, Theo. They were wonderful children. She and Justice encouraged them to learn. Besides making sure they both did their homework, Bessie tried to supplement their knowledge with stories about the people who had come before them. Great Americans like Abraham Lincoln, Harriet Tubman, and Frederick Douglass. She was pleased they enjoyed learning. Who would they become? Hard to know. But one thing she was certain of. With faith in God and an education, they had a better chance than those who had neither.

Bessie got up and took her mother's cookbook from a shelf near the stove. She brought it over to the table and handed it to her daughter. "I want you to learn how to cook every single recipe in this book. Not because I want you to get married and cook for your family, although if you do get married, it will be very useful. I want you to do this so you will have a part of your grandmother inside of you. It's important we make sure she stays alive through us. Can you understand that at all?"

Bessie wasn't sure she was getting through to her daughter. What she was trying to convey was so important. She was surprised to see tears run down Maddie's face. Then she realized her own face was wet as well. Once again she used her apron to wipe her cheeks.

"I understand, Mama," Maddie said. "I might not ever be a wife or a mother, but I love the stories you've told me about Grandmother. I want to carry her with me. And you too, Mama. I want you both to live through me." Maddie took a shaky breath. "I'm sorry I said that mean thing about you not being special, Mama. You're the most special person I've ever known."

This time Bessie didn't wipe away her tears. She just scooted her chair over, pulled her daughter to her chest, and sobbed.

Meredith and Julia stayed at the coin shop for a while after the police arrived. Officer Frett was there, along with a police detective who promised to send out a BOLO on Crystal. Knowing that the police in Savannah would be on the lookout for Crystal made Julia feel better. She was concerned for her.

Julia called Beau, who came by to pick her up and take her to church. It was youth group night, and Julia realized on the way that she hadn't had any supper.

"When we're done, let's get something to eat," she told Beau. "I'm starving. That shrimp cocktail and bread pudding were delicious, but my tummy wants something more. It'll be eight o'clock before we get out of church."

"Not a problem," Beau said with a smile. "How about picking up cheeseburgers and shakes from Peachie's?"

At that moment, Julia's stomach decided to rumble, and Beau laughed.

"I take it that's a yes?"

"You shouldn't be eating like that, you know."

Beau held up his right hand. "I promise to eat salad for my next two meals."

Julia sighed. "All right, but I'm holding you to it." She leaned over and kissed Beau on the cheek. "I wish you'd quit worrying about Grady Prescott. I'm convinced he doesn't want to harm me. He just wants to let me know he's free and that I failed in proving he was guilty of attacking those people in Atlanta. It's an ego thing."

"I'm not taking any chances," Beau said, his face tight. "I don't trust him. He's hurt people before, and he could be angry with you. That's a very dangerous combination."

Julia sighed. Beau had his mind made up, and she knew him well enough to know that he wouldn't change it…no matter what. Although she wasn't really worried about Prescott, she had to admit that having Beau around whenever she wasn't with Meredith made her feel better.

As they drove to the church, Julia kept turning the case over and over in her mind. So many people who could be involved, yet no one seemed guilty…except Crystal. Her boyfriend had to have been involved in the coin shop robbery, but was that related to the grits contest? No matter how many scenarios she considered, she kept hitting dead ends. She wanted to believe that Prescott was involved in the robbery, but nothing tied him to it. In fact, it was just the opposite. At the time of the robbery, he was at the contest. No one could be at two places at one time, could they? She felt so strongly that there was something she was missing. But what was it?

Chapter Twenty-Seven

WHEN JULIA GOT TO THE office the next morning, she was met by Carmen. "Meredith wants to see you," she said. "You won't believe this. You really won't." She turned and went back to her desk, leaving Julia to wonder what was going on.

"What now?" she asked Meredith as she entered her office.

She pushed something across her desk toward Julia. "True to his word, Ernie Prothro wrote an apology for casting aspersions toward the Downhome Diner. You'll love this."

"I guess Quin got through to him." Julia picked up the paper and saw Ernie's column, titled "Savannah's Eats and Treats." She put her purse on the desk and sat down to read it.

Last Saturday I wrote about the disastrous event on River Street called True Grits. It was a contest that was supposed to introduce us to the best grits in Savannah. Instead it proved something I've said many times in this column. Make sure you know what you're doing before trying to put together an event like this. Unfortunately, those in charge lost control, and two of the judges became sick. One of us actually ended up in the hospital.

I mentioned in my previous column that I found it odd that only one of the contestants' dishes escaped the tainted addition from a bottle labeled PAPRIKA that was actually a very dangerous hot pepper. I may have inadvertently made it sound as if they might have been responsible for what happened. However, since then I've come to realize that they were probably not involved at all. I regret the inference. The truth is, their food is tolerable and probably didn't need any additional seasoning. I understand they have their own smoked paprika mix and that this is why they chose not to use the so-called paprika set out for the contestants.

So, apologies to anyone who may have been offended by my previous column. Maybe this competition should get a second chance. I'm offering my assistance for another attempt...the right way this time.

"That man," Julia fumed.

"I know. It's a passive-aggressive apology," Meredith said with a sigh. "I wonder what Charlene will think about it."

At that moment Meredith's phone rang. She picked it up. "Charlene," she said, shaking her head.

Meredith said "Hello," and nothing much after that except, "Uh-uh." "Sure." And "I understand." When she hung up, she grimaced at Julia.

"I take it she's not crazy about the column."

"Well, would you like your restaurant's food to be rated *tolerable* to all of Savannah?"

"Of course not."

Julia was getting ready to make another comment when Carmen stepped inside the office. She held a small laptop computer in her hands. "You must see this," she said. "It's *muy bien*."

"What are we looking at?" Julia asked.

"Most people read the news online. I brought a hard copy to you so you could pass it around and cut out the column if you want to. But I've also been checking the newspaper's website. You need to see the comments section."

She put the laptop on Meredith's desk. Julia pushed her chair around the corner so she could see it too. "What is it we're supposed to be looking at?" she asked.

Carmen reached over and scrolled down the page. Then she clicked on a link. The comments section opened up.

"My goodness," Meredith said. "A lot of people seem to have an opinion about the column."

"Yes, and most of them are about the diner. People are really mad at him for calling their food 'tolerable.' People love the Downhome Diner. Ernie stepped on a lot of toes this time."

Sure enough, as Meredith scrolled through the comments, it was clear that people were upset. *The Downhome Diner is one of the best restaurants in Savannah*, one man said. *And if someone hadn't disrupted the grits contest, they would have won. Their grits are awesome!*

"And look at this one," Carmen said, leaning over the top of the desk. "This woman wants everyone who loves the diner to visit them in the next few days to show how much they're appreciated!"

"This is wonderful," Julia said. "But where were these people when the first article came out?"

Carmen straightened up. "Well, think about it. If a police detective came in here and told you he was pretty sure I stole something from you, what would you think?"

"I wouldn't believe it," Meredith said quickly.

"Wait a minute," Julia said. "I think I see where you're going with this. We might be a little concerned because it came from someone who seems trustworthy. Even though we find it hard to believe, we wouldn't just disregard it."

Carmen pointed at her as if she'd just won a contest. "Sí! Exactly. But if that detective came back and said, 'I was wrong. She's innocent.' And then he added, 'Even though she was a troubled teen and prone to stealing, I guess I got it wrong this time.'"

"I would be enraged," Julia said.

"As would I," Meredith added.

"Right. The first time the accusation seems possible, even though you don't really believe it. But the second time, even though he's telling you I'm innocent, he still finds a way to diss me."

"So the first time Ernie threw accusations at the diner," Julia said slowly, "it seemed there might be something to it because of his reputation. But when he admitted that the diner wasn't guilty of anything, he also used his apology to belittle them again."

"Sí," Carmen said. "You got it."

"Thanks, Carmen," Meredith said. "And by the way, I don't care if the governor of Georgia walked in here and told me they had video of you stealing something from us. I still wouldn't believe it."

"Thank you," Carmen said, blushing. She picked up her laptop. "I'll leave you two to it then."

"Well, this is an interesting turn of events," Meredith said after Carmen left.

"You mean the diner's loyal customers deciding to respond to what they perceive as an attack against them, and suddenly the Downhome Diner is more popular than ever before?"

Meredith nodded. "My guess is that even more will add their support because they don't like to see the 'little guy' bullied by those with power."

Julia laughed. "So being involved in the grits contest is bringing in more business, but it didn't happen the way Charlene planned."

"Exactly. I predict they're going to be very busy."

"So if the diner's business suddenly increases, does that mean we're out of a job?"

"I hope not," Meredith said. "Frankly, I want to see this thing all the way through. Until Charlene tells us we're fired, we can continue to tell people we're working on behalf of the diner."

"Okay, I want to keep going too, but I have to admit I'm a little confused." Julia sighed. "So let's talk about what we know so far. There's the comment from one of the robbers that Donnie hears as *gravy*. I believe he was talking about Grady Prescott."

Meredith shook her head. "Julia, we have to let that go for now. First of all, we have no evidence linking Prescott to the robbery at the coin shop. Secondly, we have no idea what the robber was trying to say. Maybe he really did say *gravy*. You know, like they would be riding the gravy train."

Julia raised an eyebrow. "Really? The gravy train? And was the robber actually a gangster from the twenties?"

"Oh, Julia. People still talk like that."

"Maybe in old black-and-white movies," Julia mumbled.

"Look, the police didn't take that seriously, and we can't prove it's a reference to Prescott."

"You're going to ignore it?"

"No," Meredith said. "Of course not. I'm just saying that we can't do anything with that yet. So let's put it on a shelf and move on to what we're sure of. Just for now, okay?"

"Okay," Julia said.

"Well, we know that Crystal…what's her last name?"

Julia reached down for her purse and took out her notebook. "Sullivan."

"That's right. Sullivan. We pretty much know from her behavior that she was involved in the coin shop robbery. She obviously told someone about the valuable coin and when it would be in the shop."

"I feel sorry for Dale," Julia said. "He just couldn't believe one of the people he'd treated so well would turn on him."

"I know. It may take him a while to recover from her betrayal." Meredith paused and took a deep breath. "I'm certain her boyfriend was behind the actual robbery. That's why she was able to buy the ring. He sold the coin to someone through the black market and gave Crystal the money to get the ring."

Julia frowned. "But why is she still here? Shouldn't she have taken off with him?"

"Maybe they're waiting around for a while so it won't look suspicious when they leave? Or maybe they haven't actually sold the coin yet. Maybe they're waiting on the buyer."

"That could be it," Julia said slowly. "You know, when I was in Atlanta, we had a couple of cases where the thief got inside information from a girlfriend. But once he got the money he took off and left her behind."

"But if he bought her that ring…"

"He could be buying her off." Julia leaned forward. "Or he's just trying to keep her happy while he gets away. Maybe he wrote her a bad check. If so, the jewelry store should find that out before long."

"If Crystal really has been left behind, or if she finds out the money he gave her for the ring isn't real, she might be more willing to talk to us."

"I think you're right," Meredith said. "But first we have to find her."

Chapter Twenty-Eight

JULIA AND MEREDITH SPENT THE rest of the morning trying to locate Crystal Sullivan. Dale had given them Crystal's address, as well as the names, addresses, and phone numbers of the people she'd listed as contacts on her employment application. Even though she hadn't shown up since leaving the shop, Dale was still holding out hope. Julia felt sorry for him.

Julia and Meredith made several calls. One of the numbers on Crystal's application belonged to her mother. So far every time they got someone on the phone who might be able to help, they discovered the police had already talked to them. When Meredith got off the phone she told Julia the same was true with Crystal's mother.

"I can't say I'm unhappy that the police have already talked to these people," she said. "That means they're doing their job."

"So what did Crystal's mother say?" Julia asked.

"She claims she has no idea where Crystal is or whether or not she was involved in the robbery. She hasn't talked to Crystal in almost four years. Said when she left home at eighteen, Crystal told her she'd never hear from her again. So far she's kept that promise."

"Well, that's sad," Julia said.

"Frankly, she couldn't have seemed less interested in what her daughter was up to," Meredith said. "I can't understand not caring about your own child."

"So a dead end there?"

"Yeah, it seems so."

"What about the other contacts?"

"I called her brother in Atlanta," Meredith said, "who sounds just as concerned about Crystal as her mother. There's one name left on the list. An aunt who lives in Savannah."

"I'm sure the police have called her too."

Meredith nodded. "Probably, but I want to make sure we've done everything we can." She stared at Julia for a moment before saying, "We're running out of steam, you know. If this aunt can't help us, I don't know where to go next."

"Remember that tomorrow night we're having dinner at Sharrah's. Maybe that will yield something."

"What was it Jerome told us about Cyrus?"

Julia thought for a moment. "Jerome said Cyrus was the only one there when he delivered the paprika…"

"Which means Cyrus could have substituted the jar without anyone seeing him."

Julia felt a prickle of hope. "Come to think of it, that's probably the only time the jar could have been tampered with or exchanged. Not long after that the contestants would be at their tables, preparing their dishes."

"You're right." Meredith frowned.

"You don't look very interested in that possibility."

"It's not that. I just realized we've left a stone unturned." She looked at Julia. "Jerome said the letter and the jar of paprika were left for him at A Cup of Jo."

Julia snapped her fingers. "We should have talked to someone there to see if they could confirm that information. If Jerome lied, that could mean that he's responsible for the pepper."

"Let's run over there now and see if anyone remembers who dropped it off."

Julia grabbed her purse and told Carmen they were leaving. The women hurried out the back door and got into Meredith's car. About fifteen minutes later they were parking the car on River Street. When they got to A Cup of Jo, they looked around for Jo McAllister. As they ordered coffee, she came out from the back and Julia called her over.

After introducing themselves they asked if they could speak to her a moment.

"You say you're from Magnolia Investigations?" Jo asked. She was a thin woman with golden blond hair and bright green eyes. Her mouth had permanent laugh lines. Julia liked her immediately.

"Yes," Julia said with a smile.

"Then you work with Carmen Lopez?" she asked.

Meredith nodded. "Yes, we do."

"One of my best customers," Jo said. "What can I do for you?"

Julia looked around and realized there were several people standing near them. "Could we talk over there?" she asked, gesturing to a small table at the back of the room.

"Sure."

The barista, a young man with a friendly smile said, "Go ahead and sit. I'll bring your drinks as soon as they're ready."

"That's so nice," Julia said. "Thank you."

"Happy to do it."

They joined Jo at the table, where she'd already sat down. "Does this have anything to do with the grits competition Friday night?" she asked as the women took their seats.

"Why, yes," Julia said. "How did you know?"

"The police stopped by and asked some questions. Since you're investigators, it only makes sense."

"May I ask what the police wanted?" Meredith asked.

"They wanted to know about a letter and a package dropped off here for Jerome Matheson, the chef at Mama Louise's Kitchen."

"Do you mind if we ask what you told them?" Julia asked.

"Of course not. I'll tell you exactly what I told them. I'm afraid you're not going to like it though."

"Go ahead," Julia said.

Before Jo could answer, the barista came over with two cups of coffee. He set them on the table. "Can I get you anything else?" he asked.

"I don't think so," Meredith said. "Thank you so much."

He gave them a wide smile. "Sure. If you need something else just let me know."

As he walked away, Meredith said, "What a nice young man."

"Yes, he is," Jo said. "I only employ friendly people. There's enough sadness and anger in the world. I try to make this a little oasis. Somewhere people can come and relax."

"I think you've succeeded," Julia said. "I love the ambience in here."

"Thank you. Now back to your question," Jo said. She sighed. "The truth is, I was so busy with all the people heading to the grits contest that I never noticed the package or the letter. I can't tell you anything about it."

"Oh dear," Meredith said. "Did the police ask your employees about it?"

"Actually, they didn't. The young woman working the counter that day wasn't here when they questioned me."

"And the police never came back to question her?"

"No. I asked Marcie to call them, but I don't think she has yet."

"I don't suppose Marcie's here now," Julia said.

The lines around Jo's eyes crinkled as she smiled. "Yes, she is. Would you like to talk to her?"

Meredith nodded. "Very much."

Jo stood. "I'll send her over." She pointed at their cups. "How's the coffee?"

Julia, who'd ordered Carmen's favorite coffee, Mucho Mocha, smiled. "It's wonderful. Carmen has great taste."

Jo nodded. "Yes, she does. And what did you get?" she asked Meredith.

Julia watched as Meredith grinned. She looked a little embarrassed. "I just got the morning blend. Nothing fancy, although Julia's coffee smells so good."

Jo leaned down and lowered her voice. "Don't tell anyone, but I actually like my coffee black. Especially in the morning. I have to work up to some of the flavored coffees. Love 'em, but when I first get here, all I want is a straight shot of caffeine. The morning blend is my go-to coffee." She straightened up, her expression friendly. "I'll get Marcie. It was nice meeting you both. Hope you come back."

"Thank you, Jo," Julia said. "We will."

"I can see why Carmen likes this place," Meredith said as Jo walked away. "The coffee's great and the people are so friendly and warm."

"This is nice, isn't it? I would like to come back too." Anticipation of a possible breakthrough bubbled up inside Julia. "So we finally get to talk to someone the police haven't seen yet."

"It's not a competition," Meredith said.

"I know that, but I'd like to prove to Officer Frett that I'm not off my nut and I'm certainly not stalking Grady Prescott."

Meredith took a sip of coffee and then said, "Well, let's pray this Marcie person can finally give us a lead. If we can find out who wrote the letter, I think we'll finally start to see some light at the end of a very long tunnel."

Chapter Twenty-Nine

A FEW MINUTES LATER, A girl with short hair that was dyed bright red walked over to their table. "I'm Marcie," she said. "Jo told me you wanted to talk to me?"

"Yes, please sit down," Meredith said, gesturing to the empty chair next to her.

Marcie slid into the chair. "You're interested in the person who dropped off the letter and package Friday night?"

"Yes," Julia said. "Did you recognize him?"

"No. So many customers come through here. We have regulars, but most of our business is from tourists. Events like the grits contest mean we get really busy."

"Can you describe this person?" Meredith asked.

"I think so. It was a man. Probably in his thirties. Brown hair. Nice looking." She shrugged.

"What did he say?" Julia asked.

"He told me that the letter and the package would be picked up by Jerome Matheson. Jerome comes here almost every day. I also knew him because of his restaurant. My family loves... Well, used to love...Mama Louise's Kitchen. Before the prices got so high."

"Did this man say anything else?"

"He gave me a twenty-dollar bill for helping him. I tried to return it, but he wouldn't take it."

"I don't suppose he told you his name?" Julia asked.

Marcie shook her head. "He just thanked me and left."

"Is there anything else you can tell us about him?" Meredith asked.

"I'm sorry. No."

Julia took a sip of her coffee. "What did you do with the items he gave you?"

"I kept them behind the counter and told the other baristas that Mr. Matheson would be coming in and that we needed to make sure he got them."

"So did he come in Friday morning and pick them up?" Meredith asked.

"Yes, he was here. I waited on him. He was surprised to learn there was something here for him. I gave him the letter and the package after taking his coffee order."

"And what did he do?" Julia asked.

"He moved over to the side of the counter so the next person could place their order. While he was waiting for his coffee, he read the letter. Then he opened the package and tasted what was in the jar. It couldn't possibly have been hot pepper."

"How can you be sure?"

"Because if it was some kind of really hot pepper, he would've had some kind of reaction, right? But he just put the lid back on and stuck the jar and the letter in his pocket. He waited for his coffee, and then he left. He was acting normally. That's all there was to it."

Marcie confirmed everything Jerome had told them. Speaking to her hadn't moved them forward at all in their investigation.

"Thank you so much for talking to us," Meredith said. "We appreciate it."

Marcie smiled. "You're welcome. If I can do anything else, please let me know."

"We will," Julia said.

As Marcie walked away, Julia sighed. "Well, everything she says agrees with what Jerome told us. As much as I hate to say it, we can take him off our list of suspects. I think—"

"Excuse me." Julia turned her head to see Marcie standing next to their table. "I just remembered something."

"What's that?" Meredith asked.

"The man who brought the jar of paprika?"

Julia nodded.

Marcie put her finger on her cheek. "He had a scar. Right here." She shrugged. "I'd forgotten about it until just now. Thought you should know."

Julia felt her heart beat faster in her chest. "Wait a minute." She reached down and grabbed her purse. She'd made a copy of Carmen's drawing. She pulled it out and unfolded it. "Does this look like the man?"

Marcie frowned at the image. "I don't know. It might be." She shook her head. "I'm sorry. When we're busy there are so many people. I just can't be sure. I think that could be him."

"Thanks again, Marcie," Meredith said.

"You're welcome." She turned and went back to work behind the counter.

Julia stared at Meredith with her mouth open. "Grady Prescott gave the jar and the letter to Matheson. It gives us a direct connection between him and what happened at the contest."

"Hold on," Meredith said, frowning. "First of all, Marcie couldn't identify him. She said the drawing of Prescott, which isn't perfect, *might* be him. She couldn't be sure. The police will never see this as evidence. It's a shaky ID at best."

Julia knew Meredith was right. "If we tried to share this with them, they'd accuse me of harassing Prescott again."

"Exactly. And there's something else," Meredith said. "Marcie said Jerome tasted the contents of the jar. Like she said, if it had been ground ghost peppers, he would have had a reaction. So even if it was Grady who gave him the jar, it was just paprika. There's nothing illegal about giving someone a spice."

"So someone brings the letter and the jar labeled PAPRIKA to Marcie," Julia said. "When Jerome comes in, she gives it to him. He reads the letter, tastes the paprika, and takes it to the contest that evening. He assumes the paprika is from Ernie, whom he trusts. The other cooks use it either because they were told Ernie would judge their efforts more highly if they sprinkled it on top of their dish or that it would look better on TV. They saw others use it and decided to follow suit. Maribelle didn't use it because she had her own paprika." She closed her eyes a moment. "Let's say that Prescott did deliver the letter and the paprika. Just for argument's sake." She opened her eyes. "Why would he do that?"

"Well, I'd say it was done to distract the police so they couldn't respond as quickly to the coin shop robbery."

"Except…," Julia said.

"Except what?" Meredith responded.

"It seems that the seasoning Jerome tasted was actually paprika. So we're back to the same question as before. When was the paprika traded for ghost pepper?"

"And why not give Jerome the pepper in the first place?"

Julia thought a moment. "Because he probably wouldn't have put the jar on the table. The person behind this had to use regular paprika at first, assuming Jerome would check it out. The pepper came later. Whoever did this had no choice."

"Yet no one sees anyone tamper with the jar."

Julia tapped her fingers on the table. "We need to eliminate the impossible...."

"Here we go with Sherlock Holmes again," Meredith said, her eyes sparkling with humor.

"Well, it works, doesn't it?"

Meredith nodded. "Yes, it does."

"So in this case, someone had to change out the jar, and it had to be done before anyone used the so-called paprika."

"When Jerome put the jar on the table, there was only one person there," Meredith said.

In unison, they said, "Cyrus Sharrah."

Chapter Thirty

WHEN THEY GOT BACK TO the office, Julia had planned to call Crystal's aunt, but her instincts told her it would be a waste of time. She got up from her desk and walked into Meredith's office.

"I get the feeling Crystal's aunt won't pick up the phone if I call. If the police have already talked to her, she may be sensitive about having anyone else question her about Crystal. And even if she does answer, it's easier to lie on the phone than when you're face-to-face with someone."

Meredith stopped what she was doing and looked up at Julia. She paused a moment before saying, "You're right. You think we should just go there?"

Julia nodded. "I really do. I also think we need to talk to Charlene again. I feel a little uncomfortable telling people we're investigating this situation for her. If her traffic has improved she might want us to drop the case. I don't want to give people the wrong impression."

"We're allowed to look into this ourselves, you know," Meredith said with a smile. "But I appreciate that you want to make sure we appear professional. I'll give her a call."

"Okay," Julia said. "But what if she says she's happy with things the way they are and wants us to stop?"

"I really don't think she will. She knows we want to find out who's behind this."

"But if she does…"

Meredith shrugged. "We'll close the case…on paper."

Julia grinned. "I've got to find out who put that hot pepper on the table. It's keeping me up at night."

Meredith laughed. "We certainly want you to get your rest. I'll write down the aunt's address and give Charlene a quick call. I'll meet you at my car."

Julia went back to her office, turned off her computer, and grabbed her purse. She told Carmen they'd be gone for a while and where they'd be. Then she went out to wait by Meredith's car. Beau and Meredith had been driving her around ever since they found out Grady Prescott was in town. She was trying to go along with it since they were both concerned about her, but she couldn't live like this forever. What if Prescott stayed in Savannah?

She tried the door to Meredith's car, but it was locked. She leaned against the door, waiting for Meredith to come out of the building. As she waited, a dark blue sedan with darkened windows drove slowly down the road next to the office building. It seemed to reduce its speed as it got closer. Julia felt a sense of panic. What if it was Prescott? And what if he was seeking revenge for her part in sending him to prison?

She was trying to decide whether she should run back into the building when the car pulled into the agency's parking area. Julia was frozen in place, unable to move or even think.

The window on the driver's side slid down slowly. With shaking fingers, Julia opened her purse and put her hand on her gun.

When the window was all the way down, Julia found herself looking into the face of an older gentleman she didn't know. He had gray hair, a small beard, and kind eyes.

"Excuse me, ma'am," he said. "I'm trying to find Abercorn Street. Can you help me?"

Julia released her grip on the gun, but she couldn't stop her body from shaking. She took a deep breath and fought to control her fear. "You…" She gulped and started again. "You're looking for the Olde Pink House?"

"Why, yes, ma'am. How did you know?"

"Just a guess. It's very popular in Savannah." Trying to keep her voice steady, Julia gave the man directions to the restaurant. It really was a special spot. The Olde Pink House was considered one of Savannah's best eating establishments.

"Thank you very much," the man said. He hesitated a moment before adding. "Are you all right, ma'am? Is there anything I can do to help you?"

Julia shook her head. "No, I'm fine. But thank you for asking."

The man put his car into gear but seemed unwilling to leave. The back door of the office building opened, and Meredith came out. She hurried down the steps and over to Julia.

"Is everything all right?" she asked.

"Yes. I'm fine." She smiled at the man, who still seemed concerned about her. Finally, he waved and drove out of the parking lot.

Meredith clicked the car's remote, and the locks popped up. "I'm so sorry. I should have unlocked the car for you. I forgot about it."

Julia quickly got into the car. Meredith slid into the driver's side. "Oh, Jules, what's wrong? You're crying."

Julia wiped away the tears that streamed down her face. "This has got to stop," she said. "I can't live my life being afraid. I seriously doubt that Grady Prescott plans to assassinate me. He only attacks old people who can't defend themselves. And even then, he's never killed anyone. Besides, if something happened to me, he'd be the first suspect. He's not going to do anything that could land him back in jail. On purpose anyway."

"Beau and I aren't trying to make you afraid," Meredith said. "We're just trying to keep you safe."

"I know that, and I love you both for it. But I need my life back. God hasn't given me a spirit of fear. I have to conquer this. Having you two take me everywhere and watch out for me constantly isn't making me stronger."

Meredith was quiet for a moment. "I understand what you're saying," she said finally, "but it's not like we're with you every second. I think the measures we're taking now are just prudent."

"Maybe. But starting tomorrow, I'm going to drive myself to work and home. I don't mind going with you if we're both headed to the same place. But if I want to check out something on my own, I'll do it. I don't need your permission."

"All right," Meredith said. "But just remember that Beau and I love you. We don't want you taking chances you don't need to take."

Julia reached out and touched Meredith's hand. "I know that. Let's just loosen the reins a little, okay?"

"Okay. You've got a deal. Now, do you still want to talk to Crystal's aunt?"

"Yes, it's fine." Julia lay her head back on the seat rest, glad to have lowered the temperature...along with her heart rate.

Chapter Thirty-One

It didn't take long to get to Crystal's aunt's house. Julia opened her eyes when she felt the car stop. They were sitting in the driveway of a Craftsman bungalow. It was obvious someone had put some work into it. The main part of the house was celery green. The front pillars were white as were the window frames and some architectural features that made the house stand out.

There was a car in the driveway. Meredith pulled in behind it. They got out and went up to the front door, and Julia rang the doorbell. Seconds later a woman opened the door and smiled at them. She was wearing a simple cotton dress, tennis shoes, and an apron. Her brownish hair was curly and her makeup light.

"Can I help you?" she asked.

"Mrs. McKenyon," Meredith said, "we're with Magnolia Investigations. We're worried about Crystal. Could we talk to you for a moment?"

The woman's smile slipped, and her expression tightened. "Well, I guess so. But I'm not sure I can help you."

"We won't take up much of your time, we promise," Julia said with a smile.

The woman held the door open. Meredith and Julia stepped into a nice living room with a fireplace and overstuffed furniture.

Three cats were curled up, two on the couch and one on a lovely chair near the cracking fire. Music played softly in the background. Julia recognized a lovely rendition of "The Old Rugged Cross."

"Please sit down," Mrs. McKenyon said. She picked up the cat lying in the chair and put him on the floor. "You have a bed, Mr. Magoo," she said. The cat gazed at her with an injured expression. He marched off with his tail held high.

Julia chuckled. "My cat acts exactly the same way. I truly believe she thinks she owns my house, and I'm a rather rude guest who doesn't know her place."

Mrs. McKenyon's face relaxed. "You have a cat? What kind?"

"She's a gray tabby. Her name is Bunny."

"Well, these three reprobates are Mr. Magoo, Mouse, and Rocky." She shook her head. "The orange one who is currently offended is Mr. Magoo. He doesn't see very well, I'm afraid. Mouse is the Siamese, and the black cat is Rocky. They're all rescues. Magoo and Mouse were at the shelter. Rocky was living outside in our neighborhood and decided one day that he was coming inside to live with me. It seems I had no say in the matter."

Julia and Meredith laughed. Julia took the chair vacated by Magoo, and Meredith sat down on the couch. She'd no sooner taken her place when Mouse got up, strolled over, and lay down on her lap. Most Siamese weren't this friendly. Meredith stroked her soft fur, and Mouse began to purr loudly.

"Seems she likes you," Mrs. McKenyon said. "She's not normally that friendly. I take a lot of stock in how my cats respond to people. You must be a nice woman."

"I try to be," Meredith said with a smile. It was obvious she was smitten with the beautiful cat. "I have a cat too. They're incredible animals."

"Can I get you a cup of coffee?" Mrs. McKenyon asked. "I keep it going all day in case I need caffeine. Made a fresh pot just before you got here."

"Thank you," Meredith said. "I'd love it."

"Me too," Julia said. Actually, she was more in the mood for something cold, but accepting a cup of coffee made it easier to stay longer.

"I'll be right back," she said. She left the room, obviously headed for the kitchen.

Once she'd gone, Julia stood up and looked around the room. Several pictures of Crystal at different ages dotted the room. She also looked for any signs Crystal was here. Nothing. She sat back down. "Looks like she's very close to Crystal. My guess is she was more a mother to her than her own mother."

"I think you're right. If anyone knows where Crystal is, it's this aunt."

A rattling sound made it clear Mrs. McKenyon was on her way back.

Sure enough she came into the room with two cups of coffee. She put one on a side table for Julia, making sure to put a coaster under it. Then she did the same thing for Meredith, setting her cup down on the coffee table. "I'll be right back," she said.

A minute or two later she returned holding her own cup and a small container stuffed with different sweeteners. "I didn't know if you wanted something in your coffee," she said. "I brought this just in case."

"Thank you," Meredith said. She picked up her cup to take a sip. Mouse stayed put. Julia couldn't help but smile at the cat who had staked her claim and had no intention of moving.

"You're welcome." Mrs. McKenyon sat down in a rocking chair on the other side of the coffee table. "You said you're with a detective agency?"

Meredith cleared her throat. "In a way. We call ourselves investigators though. People hire us to look into things. You know, like missing people. Missing personal property. A variety of things."

"Did you hear anything about the grits contest on River Street Friday night?" Julia asked.

"Yes. In fact Crystal told me about it. She said someone tried to poison some of the food?"

"Well, they weren't actually poisoned," Meredith said. "Someone substituted one ingredient for another. It made a couple of people sick."

Mrs. McKenyon frowned. "Oh my goodness. What did those poor people ingest?"

"Ground ghost peppers," Meredith said.

The woman's eyebrows rose. "Really? That's awful. Aren't they the hottest pepper in the world?"

"Actually, no," Meredith said. "There's a pepper called the Carolina Reaper that's much worse. But ghost peppers are still incredibly hot and can make people ill."

Julia watched her partner in surprise. How did she know about Carolina Reapers? She must have researched it. She was a wealth of information. Meredith was one of the smartest people Julia had ever known.

"Why in the world people would want to eat food that burns their mouths is beyond me," Mrs. McKenyon said with a sigh.

"Mrs. McKenyon," Julia said. "Can I—"

"Please. Call me Nora."

"Thank you, Nora. Like we said, we're here about your niece. She may be involved in something very serious. We want to find her and help her if we can."

"I don't understand," Nora said.

"The coin shop where she works was robbed. They had taken in a very valuable coin that no one was supposed to know about except the owner and his employees. That would include a young man named Donnie…and Crystal. Now understand, no one is accusing Crystal of anything, but it turns out she purchased a diamond engagement ring not long after the robbery. It's worth over ten thousand dollars. As you can probably understand, that makes her look a little guilty. But we really just want to talk to her. Ask her some questions that may completely clear her. Unfortunately, we may have said something that frightened her, and she took off. That's why we're here. We really just want to talk to her. See if we can find a way to help her."

Nora shook her head. "I haven't heard from her since Friday. She usually contacts me a couple of times every week. I expect a call soon."

"Nora, please have her contact us," Meredith said. "I know her boss is very worried. It's obvious he cares about her. And her coworker Donnie is very concerned as well."

Nora sighed. "Mr. Henshaw is such a nice man. He's done so much for Crystal. And Donnie…" She shook her head.

"Are you worried about Donnie?" Julia asked. She had really liked the young man and hoped he wasn't involved.

"Not the way you might think," Nora said. She picked up her coffee cup and stared at it for a moment. Then she took a deep breath. "I think Donnie cares deeply for Crystal. He's a wonderful young man."

"Has she been dating anyone?" Meredith asked.

Nora looked away from them. Then she slowly nodded. "Yes, and I don't like him. You may have found out from Dale that Crystal had a rough upbringing and got into some trouble."

"Yes, Dale mentioned that," Julia said.

Nora gave her a sad smile. "She changed after Dale and Donnie came into her life. Donnie has been there for her through thick and thin. But it's like she doesn't see him. Instead she started dating some older man she met at an event on River Street. I don't like him. He doesn't go to church and there's something…sleazy about him. Crystal told me when we talked on Friday that he bought her an expensive engagement ring."

"Do you know his name?" Julia asked.

Nora nodded. "Grady Prescott."

Chapter Thirty-Two

JULIA HAD BEEN EXPECTING TO hear Prescott's name, but she was still shocked when Nora actually said it.

"We think Mr. Prescott might be involved with the robbery at the coin shop where Crystal works," Meredith said. "Now it's even more important that she's found."

The look of distress on Nora's face made it clear she was worried about her niece. Julia believed her when she said she hadn't seen her.

"Do you have a card or something?" Nora asked. "When I hear from her, I'll call you."

"We hope you do," Meredith said, "but please contact the police first."

"But what if they arrest her before you tell her what to do?" Nora asked, fear written clearly on her face.

"We're not the police," Meredith said, handing her one of their cards. "We can't interfere. Just tell Crystal to ask the police for a lawyer. They'll send her a court-appointed attorney who will tell her the options she has. And then call us. We'll try to see her too. It's the best we can do. I'm sure Prescott has the coin now. It's possible he'll contact her, but he also might be long gone. I just don't know."

"She seemed to believe Prescott was in the army reserve, but I don't believe that," Julia said. "My guess is he's planning to take off after he sells the coin."

"But he already gave her the money for the ring," Nora said. "Wouldn't he have had to sell the coin first?"

"No." Julia looked at Meredith. "I'm glad we asked the jewelry store to hold on to that ring."

Meredith nodded.

"What do you mean?" Nora asked.

"He may have given her a bad check. It can take the bank a few days to realize it."

"She never mentioned the robbery to me." Nora frowned. "I hope she didn't help him set it up."

Julia wondered if Prescott was already gone. But who knew? He'd hung around long enough to visit her and talk to the police. Maybe he was still here. Was Crystal with him? If they could locate her, maybe they could find him too.

"I think you need to prepare yourself, Nora," Meredith said. "She may have given the thieves the information they needed to get their hands on that coin."

"I understand," Nora said. She wiped a tear from her eye. "It's so hard for me to believe she would do anything to hurt Mr. Henshaw. She's always talking about how important he is to her."

"Is there anyone else your niece hangs around with?" Meredith asked. "Male friends or family?"

"No, not really. But Grady had a couple of friends I didn't care for."

"Why is that?" Julia asked.

"They just… Well, Grady would put on this big show, you know? Trying to act like he liked me. That he cared for Crystal. But his friends were sullen. Sometimes rude. I didn't like them at all and told Crystal that. She finally told Grady they couldn't come here anymore. That was about a month ago."

"How long has Crystal known Grady?" Meredith asked.

"Not long. About six weeks maybe." She shook her head and wiped away another tear. "If she did anything wrong, it was because of Grady Prescott. That man needs to be in jail."

"I agree," Julia said. "Your niece may simply have mentioned that an expensive coin was coming into the shop. It's possible she had no idea he was going to steal it."

"I hope you're right," Nora said. "That girl was finally on the right track. I just can't stand to think that she'll end up in trouble after how hard she's worked to clean up her life."

"We hope that won't happen," Meredith said. She stood up. "Thank you for talking to us," she said. "I know this was hard on you."

Nora nodded. It was obvious she was distraught.

Meredith and Julia left, closing the front door behind them. "This is a tough one," Meredith said as they walked back to her car. "I feel bad for Nora."

"I do too," Julia said. "But I also worry about Crystal. I think it's possible she was swept off her feet by Prescott. I also think he started dating Crystal before she told him about the coin. But when it came down to a choice between a woman who loved him and money, Crystal lost. I don't know if she suspects it yet, but it won't take long before she figures it out."

They reached Meredith's car and got inside.

"You're assuming she wasn't in on it from the beginning and that she's not with him now," Meredith said.

"I guess so. I mean, I know that's possible, but I just get the feeling she's not that coldhearted. I think she really does care about Dale Henshaw, and somehow this thing just got out of control."

"You know something?" Meredith said, glancing at her. "You spent years as a prosecuting attorney. You've seen the worst of the worst, but most of the time you still give people the benefit of the doubt. I really respect that."

Julia turned to look out the window. "Not always."

"You're thinking about Grady Prescott?"

"Yeah. As a prosecutor I had to stick to the law. And the evidence. There's no wiggle room. When it came to Prescott, we had all of it. I've gone over it in my mind." She sighed. "We did the right thing. I'm sure of it."

Meredith started the car. "Good. You're one of the most fair-minded people I've ever known. You would no more send someone to prison you knew was innocent than you would turn down a Diet Dr Pepper."

Julia turned toward Meredith and burst out laughing. "Now, *that's* a great vote of confidence if I ever heard one."

Both women broke out in giggles.

"Oh, Mere," Julia said, wiping her eyes. "You know how to make me laugh, and it always makes me feel better."

"What I was trying to say is that you need to trust yourself more. Give *yourself* the benefit of the doubt."

Julia leaned back in her seat and sighed. "You're right. For an attorney that fear is always there. That you're wrong. That someone is suffering because of you. I guess when Prescott showed up it just triggered that fear."

Meredith reached over and patted Julia's shoulder. "You're a very tenderhearted person who cares deeply about justice. That's why you were an attorney and a judge and are now an investigator. Don't you realize that if you didn't care about right and wrong, you would have picked a different profession? And what about all the innocent victims who got justice because of you? The people you've helped? The kids whose lives you changed when you worked as a judge in juvenile court? Do they matter?"

"Of course they do."

"Then you need to start thinking about them," Meredith said gently. "Grady Prescott caused his own problems. They had nothing to do with you."

Julia was quiet as she considered Meredith's words. Why did she tend to concentrate more on her faults and perceived mistakes than she did on the good things she'd done? She certainly wasn't the only person who did this. She'd seen young people in her courtroom who felt so defeated because of the way they looked, or something they'd done, that they'd begun to hate themselves. Sometimes they saw themselves through the eyes of careless or abusive parents. Yet she'd observed good qualities in them that made her want to give them a second chance. Why was she harder on herself than anyone else?

"Okay. I get the message," she said, smiling at Meredith. "You're right. And thanks."

"You're welcome. I'm sure Beau would have told you the very same thing."

"I agree."

"Good. I'm glad we got that straight. Now call Beau before he leaves to pick you up and tell him I'm driving you home."

"Yes, ma'am."

"Oh, and I almost forgot. Charlene says we're still on the case until we find out what really happened. So you can relax."

Julia sighed. "Good. I'm determined to find the truth. Maybe I can get some sleep then."

"We'll get there. I think we're close."

As she phoned Beau Julia thanked God she had people in her life who didn't always tell her what she wanted to hear, but told her the things she needed to hear. She was relieved that they'd made some progress today. She agreed with Meredith. She felt as if they were almost there. That the truth was just around the corner.

Chapter Thirty-Three

FRIDAY MORNING MEREDITH CALLED OFFICER Frett, who confirmed that Dale Henshaw had called him. After talking for several minutes, she hung up.

"So what's up?" Julia asked. She was in Meredith's office, waiting to see what the police had to say.

"Basically he's on the same page we are. He agrees that Crystal is probably a pawn. I told him that if we heard from Crystal we'd talk her into getting in touch with him. The case is in the hands of one of their detectives, but Officer Frett says the detective is probably willing to make a deal with Crystal if she can lead them to Prescott."

"Good." Julia sighed. "Now we just need to hear from her. I wish we knew where to look."

"This won't make you happy. The police found an address for Prescott. It's an apartment. They went by there but it was empty. He's obviously moved out."

"So he could be anywhere. Oh, Meredith, I don't want him to get away. He needs to pay for what he's done."

"I agree. By the way, I noticed you drove yourself to work this morning. How did you talk Beau into that?"

"It wasn't easy," Julia said. "I told him I couldn't go on being afraid of Prescott, and he finally understood. Besides, I'm the least of

Prescott's worries. He needs to make his deal and get out of town. He doesn't have time to mess with me." Julia clasped her hands. "I'm certain he used me as a way to make it look as if he couldn't have possibly robbed the jewelry store. My guess is he saw me at the contest and decided then to set me up. He took my wallet and dropped it in the parking lot, counting on someone finding it and trying to use one of the credit cards. Then when I told the police I thought he was the person who took it, I'd look as if I was trying to persecute him. It was the perfect way to make the police look in another direction."

"Everything certainly fell into place for him," Meredith said.

Julia shrugged. "He wanted me to recognize him when he bumped into me. Then later when I realized my wallet was gone, he counted on me calling the police."

"It took Carmen's sketch to make that part of his plan come together."

Julia nodded. "Then when someone else was caught with my wallet, Prescott ended up looking like the victim, and I was the crazy lady who was trying to send him back to jail."

"It's diabolical, really." Meredith looked at her through narrowed eyes. "Do you think he's the one who put the ghost pepper on the table?"

"It would make sense. He wanted a reason for the police to be somewhere else during the robbery at the coin shop, but..."

"I know. It doesn't feel quite right. How would he know about Ernie Prothro? Or that putting paprika on grits was something many cooks did?"

"That's what I was thinking too," Julia said. She folded her arms across her chest. "Could he have had help? Could someone have been working with him?"

"But who?"

"That's the big question. Was there someone else in on the theft? I'm pretty sure the two friends Nora mentioned are the men who broke into the coin shop."

"Yeah, that's what I was thinking," Meredith said. "But until they're found, there's no way of knowing for sure."

"So tonight we'll try to talk to Cyrus. He was left alone with the jar of paprika. I think he's the only one who could have changed it out for the jar of ghost pepper."

"He certainly could have done it. He had the opportunity. So you think he was working with Prescott?"

"But how would he know him?" Julia asked. "Prescott's been in prison for years. Not easy to make friends there." She sighed. "I don't know. I wish the police would call and tell me they've found him. I'm so afraid he'll get away. He can hide out for a long time on the money from that coin."

"If he's dividing it evenly between himself and his accomplices, it's not as much as you might think."

"You're right," Julia said. "He'll probably leave town and plan another job in a different city. I just hope he doesn't hurt anyone."

"You mean the way he did the last time?"

Julia nodded. "I'm convinced he was guilty then."

"What about now?"

"My gut tells me he's involved, but we need more than that to send him back to prison. I've put Prescott in God's hands and prayed for justice. I'm also praying for Crystal. I'm really worried about her."

"I wish I knew where she was," Meredith said. "The longer she's missing, the more concerned I get."

Julia started to say something but was interrupted by Carmen, who stuck her head in the door. "That woman is on the phone. You know, Crystal Sullivan's aunt?"

"Okay, thanks," Meredith said. "Wow. Good timing," she said to Julia. She picked up the phone.

Julia clasped her hands, hoping this call would bring good news. She listened as Meredith talked.

"Okay, we're on our way." Meredith said goodbye and hung up. "Crystal is at Nora's house. She wants to turn herself in, but she's afraid. She wants us to go with her. Is that all right?"

"As long as she's going straight to the police, I think it's fine," Julia said. She stood up. "Let's go."

It didn't take long to reach Nora's house. This time there were two cars in the driveway. Julia assumed the second one was Crystal's.

They got out of the car and hurried up the stairs to the front door. Before Julia could ring the bell, the door opened. Nora stood there with a worried look on her face.

"Thank you so much for coming," she said. "Crystal is afraid. I tried to get her to let me drive her to the police station, but she wants to speak to you first." She swung the door open, and Julia and Meredith went inside.

Crystal was sitting on the couch, crying.

Julia went over and sat down next to her while Meredith took a seat in the chair next to the couch. Nora stood behind Meredith's chair.

"I told her what you said," Nora began. "She's so scared. Afraid of going to prison."

"Tell me what happened," Julia said. "Everything you can think of."

Crystal began gasping for air.

"She's having an anxiety attack," Julia said. "Do you have a paper bag?"

Nora nodded and ran into the kitchen. She brought back a lunch-sized paper bag, which Julia opened and handed to Crystal. "Breathe into this, Crystal," she said. "Keep it over your nose and mouth. Take deep breaths."

Crystal put the sack over her mouth and nose and began doing as Julia instructed her.

"Now slow down," Julia said. "In and out. In and out." Julia began to breathe with her until her breathing became normal. Finally, Crystal removed the bag from her face.

"I'm so sorry," she said, tears running down her face. "I've made a huge mistake. I thought Grady loved me. But now I know he stayed with me because I told him about the coin." Her brown eyes darted back and forth between the three of them. "I can't believe I let Dale down after everything he's done for me."

"Can you start from the beginning?" Meredith asked gently. "From the time you met Prescott...I mean, Grady."

She nodded, her body still shivering with emotion. "I met him at a concert on River Street. He came up to me and my girlfriend and started asking us about things to do in Savannah. He said he'd just moved here." She took a deep breath. "We ended up talking almost all night. He seemed so nice." She sobbed again but this time managed to calm herself quickly. "We started going out. Then one night I mentioned the coin." Her eyes sought Julia's. "I don't know why I told him. I guess because it was interesting. I realize now that's when he decided to steal it. I had no idea. I really didn't. He started asking questions about the coin shop. As time went on I started to worry that he was up to something, but I talked myself out of it. I was convinced he would never do anything wrong. Then a few days before the shop was robbed, he told me he was in the army reserve and had to leave the country for a month. But before he left he wanted to ask me if I'd marry him." She wiped the tears from her face. "I said yes. I thought we were in love. He gave me a check for twelve thousand dollars and asked me to go ahead and find the engagement ring I wanted. I told him I could wait until he got back, but he said it was really important to him that I have a ring right away. So I deposited the check in my checking account and went to the jewelry store a few doors down. I bought a beautiful ring." She took a deep, shuddering breath. "The ring was a little too large for me so the store said they would size it. It's still there."

"Was that the day before the robbery?" Meredith asked.

Crystal nodded. "Friday morning when I went to work I was happy. All the worries I'd had about Grady were gone. He wanted to marry me. I was convinced I'd been paranoid. I…I'd never had anyone ask to marry me before." She began to sob again.

Julia looked at Nora. "Can you get her something to drink, please?"

Nora nodded. "I put some coffee on. I'll get her a cup."

Julia reached for a tissue from a box on the coffee table. "Here," she said, handing it to Crystal.

"Thank you," she said. "I'm so sorry about this. It's all my fault. I should have realized the type of person he was."

"Crystal, it's not your fault," Julia said. "It's Prescott's fault. It's the fault of the men who helped him by robbing the shop. Please don't beat yourself up for something that was out of your control." She glanced over at Meredith, who nodded encouragingly at her.

Nora came back into the room with a cup that she carried over to the coffee table and put down in front of her niece. Then she sat on the couch next to Crystal and put her arm around her.

"It will be all right. You just tell these ladies what happened. Then we'll go to the police and talk to them." Nora looked up. "Will you stay with us?"

"We'll go with you," Meredith said. "But we have to let the police do their jobs. They're trying to do the right thing." She smiled at Crystal. "Don't be afraid of them. They are only looking for the truth."

Crystal nodded. "Okay," she whispered.

"So can you tell me what happened Friday night?" Julia asked.

"We were closing up when two men came into the shop. They had guns. And…" Crystal put her hand to her mouth.

"Go on," Meredith said.

"I knew who they were immediately. Grady's two deadbeat friends, Jerry and Shawn."

Julia's ears pricked. "Do you know where Jerry and Shawn live?"

"Shut up, Crystal," a deep voice said.

Julia turned to see Grady Prescott walk out of the kitchen. He was holding a gun aimed straight at her.

Chapter Thirty-Four

"GRADY!" CRYSTAL SAID. "WHAT ARE you doing?"

"I followed her here," he said, gesturing toward Julia with the pistol. "I didn't want her draggin' you into all this."

"It's too late for that," Julia said. "She's in a lot of trouble. And so are you."

"You don't have anything on me," he said. "You're my alibi. I can prove I wasn't involved in that robbery." He shrugged. "I guess Jerry and Shawn heard about the coin and decided to steal it. Had nothin' to do with me."

His sly smile irritated Julia. "You might think you're in the clear," she said. "But you're not."

Prescott sighed. "There you go, harassing me again. Blaming me for things I didn't do. It's sad."

"And your excuse for bringing a gun here and pointing it at us?"

He shrugged. "You threatened me." His gaze swung to Crystal. "Maybe you threatened her too. I just came back to take her with me."

"Grady, stop it," Crystal said. "You planned that robbery. I didn't tell Jerry and Shawn about the coin. I only told you." She sobbed and shook her head. "I wish I could take that back. It never occurred to me that you'd try to steal it." She looked up at him. "I thought you were a nice guy. And I believed you loved me. How could I have been so stupid?"

Prescott's intimidating expression suddenly changed. "You're not stupid. I do love you. I want you to come with me."

Crystal's mouth dropped open. "Come with you? Where? The police are going to be looking for you. I don't want that kind of life."

For the first time since she'd first met Prescott, Julia saw something besides antagonism in his face. He was hurt. He really did care for Crystal. Julia was surprised.

"When you love someone, you don't take something they said in confidence and use it for your own benefit," Julia said. "And what about Dale Henshaw? Crystal cares about him. You know that."

"But he has insurance," Prescott said. "It won't hurt him at all."

"It isn't just the money. It has to do with trust. Reputation. Not everything is about money."

"Dale was hurt, Grady," Crystal said. "He thinks I betrayed him. I hate that. He…he helped me. Gave me a job when no one else would. He's important to me. What you did was wrong. You not only hurt Dale, you hurt me. I trusted you."

Prescott shrugged. "I wasn't tryin' to hurt you, Crystal. I just wanted some money so we could take off. Go somewhere else and start a new life."

"But you left without talking to me. Just took off. I had no idea where you were. I thought you just wanted to get rid of me."

Prescott actually looked surprised. "But I gave you the money for the ring. I asked you to marry me. I meant it."

Crystal didn't say anything for a moment. Nora reached over and put her hand on Crystal's shoulder. "This just isn't right, honey," she said. "You know that. I realize you want someone to love. God has someone special for you, Crystal. But it isn't Grady. Surely you can see that."

Crystal reached up and put her hand on her aunt's. "I do," she said softly. "I'm sorry, Grady, but I don't want to start a life with someone who is trying to build it on lies. Theft. That's not the way I want to live."

The vulnerability Julia had seen on Prescott's face vanished, and the smug, self-centered man she'd first met in Atlanta was back. "Fine. I don't care." He waved his gun around. "Put all your cell phones on the coffee table."

Slowly everyone followed his instructions. He reached over, picked them up, and stuffed them in his jacket pocket. "You won't call the police for at least an hour. If you do, I'll come find you and make you sorry. Do you understand?"

Julia, Nora, and Meredith nodded, but Crystal just sat there, staring at him.

"I'm takin' off, and no one will ever find me. And I'll be livin' large while you dopes keep workin' hard and not gettin' anywhere."

"Please," Julia said. "Don't make it worse. Turn yourself in now. You don't really want to live your life looking over your shoulder all the time. Being afraid to leave the house because you'll be spotted."

Prescott laughed. "I know how to change my appearance. I also know a place to live where no one will be lookin' for me." His voice took on a pleading tone. "We can be happy, Crystal. I promise. Please, please come."

Notes from Prescott's files for the case in Atlanta suddenly jumped into Julia's mind. He had grown up in a very dysfunctional family. His mother died of a drug overdose when he was five. His father was mean and abusive. He was in and out of trouble with the juvenile division before he turned eighteen. She suddenly felt a deep wave of compassion for him.

"Grady," she said, "if you really love Crystal, you'll leave her here. She hasn't done anything wrong. The police won't charge her. But if she goes with you, that could change. Do you want her to live the kind of life you have? Don't you want more than that for her?"

Grady stood there for a few moments. Tears filled his eyes. "Okay. You're right," he said, his voice choking. He fastened his eyes on Crystal. "Always remember that I love you," he said. "And I always will." He wiped his eyes with his free hand then waved the gun around. "Remember what I said. One hour. I mean it. If anyone contacts the police before that, they'll be sorry. And so will their families."

"Grady," Crystal said, "I can't believe you'd really use that gun. Please put it down. I'll stand by your side no matter what happens."

He hesitated for a moment, as if actually considering what she said. But then he shook his head. "I'm sorry, Crystal, but I can't do that. I can't go back to prison. I really can't."

"But you haven't hurt anyone," Julia said. "You'll only be charged with robbery. You still have a chance to live a life outside of prison. If you keep running, though, I can't promise anything."

He glared at her with a look that chilled her. Hate had possessed him.

"Gerald Turano is an idiot. I can't trust him."

"What do you mean?" Julia asked.

"He was happy to plead guilty to something I did because he didn't want to die. But I can't trust him to keep quiet. Eventually he'll tell the truth." He shook his head, and his expression softened. "If I could start over, I would. But I can't."

Julia felt something touch her foot. She looked down to see her purse. Meredith had pushed it over to her. Could she get her gun out and stop him? Keep him here until the police arrived? But what if she couldn't get the gun quickly enough? Or if Grady pointed his gun at someone else in the room, threatening them as a way to get Julia to put her gun down? There were too many things that could go wrong. She pushed her purse back toward Meredith and shook her head slightly to let her know she didn't want her gun. She'd rather everyone walk away from this alive.

Grady looked at Crystal again, his gaze staying on her for several seconds. Then he walked out of the room. They heard the kitchen door close behind him.

"I can't believe I didn't lock that door," Nora said, her voice shaking. "I'm certainly going to do it from now on."

"Nora, do you have a landline?" Meredith asked.

"Yes, there's one in the kitchen." She got up and hurried toward the back of the house. They heard a sound that told them Nora had locked the back door. A moment later she came back into the room. "He's taken the phone. Just left the charger. I don't have any other phones in the house." She came back to the couch, sat down, and put her arm out so Crystal could lean against her. The girl was crying again, obviously shaken.

"Do you know your neighbors?" Meredith asked.

"Yes."

"We need to call the police right away," Julia said. "Can you go to one of them and ask to use their phone? Or just ask them to call the police?"

Crystal raised her head. "But Grady said to wait an hour. I think we need to do that."

Meredith sighed. "Honey, he's not out there, and he's not coming back. He's only thinking about getting away. We need to stop him."

"No." Crystal looked at her with wide eyes. "He'll hurt one of us if we don't do what he said. Please stay here. We'll go to the neighbors in an hour."

"He's not out there, Crystal," Julia said a little more firmly. She looked at Nora. "Which neighbor?" she asked.

Nora took a deep breath. "The Sampsons to the east of us. Very nice people. They'll help us."

"Do you want to talk to them, Nora? Or would you rather have me go?" Julia asked.

Crystal began to cry harder and held on to her aunt's arm.

"I'll go," Julia said.

"Why don't you let me talk to them?" Meredith asked.

Julia shook her head. "It might not make sense, but I want to be the one to send the police after him. He's been playing me for too long."

"I get it," Meredith said. "But take this. Please."

She handed Julia her purse, and Julia took it. "Thanks," she said. She was about as sure as she could be that Grady was gone, but she was also aware that he was unbalanced. He believed himself to be in love with Crystal. That put a kink in everything. She wasn't certain just what he would do next.

She stood up, her purse under her arm, and stepped outside, looking to the right and to the left. Then she gazed at the houses across the street. When she felt safe she jogged quickly to the house Nora had suggested. Thankfully, someone was home. She quickly explained to the woman who answered the door that a man had broken into Nora's house and held her, her niece, and her friends at gunpoint and asked her to please call the police. Although the woman Julia assumed was Mrs. Sampson didn't let her in, she got her phone and dialed 911 from behind her screen door so Julia could hear the call and provide information for the officers if asked. When the call was complete, Julia thanked her. Then she hurried back to the house to let everyone know the police were on their way. After that she went back outside, sat down on the steps, and burst into tears.

Chapter Thirty-Five

JULIA AND MEREDITH SPENT THE rest of the day talking to the police. After telling them everything they could, they were finally released to go home. Although she was still emotional, Crystal had pulled herself together and talked to the detective who showed up not long after the officers appeared. She seemed to understand that Crystal wasn't involved in the theft. That she'd been a tool in the hands of a criminal. After the detective assured them all that Crystal wasn't going to be arrested, Julia and Meredith left.

Once they were in the car and driving back to the office, Meredith said, "I'll call and cancel our reservations at Sharrah's for tonight."

"Why?" Julia asked.

"It's been a rather stressful day," Meredith said with a smile. "I assumed you'd rather have a peaceful night at home with Beau. Besides, he may not let you out of the house until Grady Prescott is in jail."

Julia shook her head and sighed. "If Grady had wanted to hurt me, he could have easily done it this afternoon. Right now he's trying to stay off the radar and get out of town."

"I agree," Meredith said, "but let's wait and see what Beau says."

"We need to keep going. Cyrus Sharrah is our last interview. The last chance we have of figuring out what happened at the True Grits competition. I know Prescott had something to do with it." She put her hand to her forehead. "Oh my goodness. Why didn't I ask him about that? It was the perfect opportunity."

Meredith took her eyes off the road for a moment to look at Julia. Her mouth hung open. "Could it be because he was holding a gun on us and you were a tiny bit distracted?"

"I guess so."

"What are you thinking about, Jules?"

Julia was quiet for a moment. She had so many thoughts running through her head. Grady's admission that he was guilty of the crime in Atlanta, feelings of compassion for him, and anger at the things he'd put Crystal, Dale, and Donnie through, along with Charlene, Maribelle, and the Downhome Diner. "I want Grady Prescott in jail," she said softly. "He can't be out in society. He's dangerous and he won't stop committing crimes. Yet part of me feels sorry for him. I don't want to, but I do. And I'm upset about what he put Crystal through. But there's nothing I can do about any of that right now. I wish I could. The other thing I'm thinking, perhaps the most important thing, is that we were hired to clear the Downhome Diner's name. We haven't done that yet. If we don't talk to Cyrus, we'll have left a stone unturned. I don't want to do that. Let's finish this out by looking under that last stone, okay?"

"Okay. Quin and I will meet you there at seven. If something happens..."

"It won't. Like I said, if Grady really wanted to hurt me, he would have done it when he had the chance."

"This is the first time I've heard you call him Grady," Meredith said. "Usually you just call him Prescott. What's changed?"

Julia considered this. "I don't know. I guess I saw a human being today, and now he seems more like *Grady*. Don't get me wrong, I want him caught and prosecuted—but I was reminded today that criminals are still people."

"People who decide to break the law and who hurt others."

Julia nodded. "You're right. I didn't care how they caught him before. But now I want them to take him alive."

"He'll spend a long time in prison."

"I know," Julia said, "but at least he'll be alive. There are lots of different outreaches to people in prison, you know? If Grady goes back to the prison he was in before, I can call the head of prison outreach there and ask him to visit Grady."

"Julia, you're a rare and wonderful person. I'm so glad you're my friend."

"This has been an unusual case," she said softly. "I spent so much time worrying that I'd been wrong about Grady. In the end I found out I was right. But it turns out that wasn't the biggest lesson I learned."

"And what was that?"

"I spent so much time feeling guilty. Worrying that I'd done something that had sent an innocent person to prison. But all that worrying didn't accomplish a thing. Didn't help anyone. Especially me. Casting your care on the Lord isn't weakness. It's strength. Somehow knowing that made it easier to have compassion for myself...and for Grady."

"I'd say that was a huge lesson," Meredith said.

Julia nodded. She couldn't have agreed more.

***

Julia and Beau got to Sharrah's on River Street a little before seven. Although Beau had been upset about the confrontation with Grady, in the end he agreed with Julia's view that he wasn't a danger to her.

After giving their car to the valet, Julia and Beau stepped inside the restaurant. The decor was striking but too modern for Julia's taste. Tables and chairs were white with metal legs. A lot of light wood panels on the walls, each one with a large, stylish *S* in the middle were the only decoration. Overhead lights were bare bulbs dangling on silver-colored cords. The floors were a brownish tile. The only real color in the restaurant came from the plates. They were blue, red, orange, green, and yellow with matching bowls and glasses. Everyone had a different colored setting. Julia found it irritating, but Sharrah's was a hit in Savannah.

The hostess led them to a table where Meredith and Quin were already waiting. Back near the kitchen was a large grill where the cooks grilled steaks, chicken, salmon, and shrimp. Julia had to admit that the aroma was captivating. The food at Sharrah's was fabulous.

"Seems you ladies had quite a day today," Quin said when they sat down. "I'm grateful you're all right."

"Well, it was certainly interesting," Julia said, smiling.

"Do you think they'll catch this Prescott person?" he asked.

"I don't know," Julia said. "I hope so. I asked the detective assigned to the case if they'd been able to find Jerry and Shawn,

Grady's friends. He thinks those aren't their real names. So far, they haven't had any luck finding them."

"That's probably where Grady is," Meredith said. "With them."

"If they haven't already left the state," Julia added.

Beau cleared his throat. "I'm not the conversation police, but I wonder if we could give Grady Prescott and his friends a rest for a while. I think we could all use some time away from them. A night off."

Julia smiled and leaned against her husband. "I think that's a marvelous idea."

Quin looked a little confused. "I thought you'd come here so you could talk to Cyrus Sharrah. Ask him about the grits competition."

Meredith laughed. "Yes, that's true. Maybe we can ignore Grady Prescott...except when we talk to Cyrus."

"Okay," he said slowly.

"Just go with it," Beau said with a grin. "It makes life so much easier."

Quin laughed. "Gotcha."

The waiter, Thomas, took their drink order and handed them menus. Meredith asked, "Is Cyrus here tonight?" Although Cyrus had started out as the chef when the restaurant opened, now he had chefs he'd trained who did the actual cooking. Julia hadn't been surprised though, when he took on the cooking duties at the grits contest. Cyrus liked seeing his name in print and his face on TV.

"Yes, he is," Thomas said. "Did you wish to speak to him?"

"If he's not too busy."

Thomas smiled. "He usually tries to say hello to every customer. Sometimes that's not possible, but I'm sure he'd be happy to stop by and talk to you."

"Thank you, Thomas," Meredith said.

As Thomas walked away, she said, "Well, that was easy."

"The last time we were here, he stopped by our table to ask if we were enjoying our dinner," Beau said. "It wasn't an in-depth discussion, but I thought it added a nice personal touch to the experience of dining here."

"Sounds good," Quin said, "but I don't like restaurants with really chatty waiters. I appreciate their effort, but when I go out, I want to talk to my friends...or whoever I'm with. Not spend my evening having a conversation with someone I don't know."

"I agree sometimes it goes too far," Meredith said.

Julia looked through the menu and decided on the brown sugar and mustard-glazed salmon with asparagus while Beau decided on the ribeye with bourbon cream sauce. They had just closed their menus when Cyrus Sharrah came strolling up to their table, a big smile on his face. He was one of the youngest chefs in Savannah, still in his twenties. His dark, debonair good looks made him one of the city's most popular bachelors.

"Good evening," he said. "Thomas tells me you'd like to speak with me?"

"Yes," Meredith said. "We're sorry to bother you on such a busy night, but we had a couple of questions to ask you about the grits contest on River Street last week."

His smile definitely dimmed some. "I don't understand. What kind of questions?"

Julia wondered if the vision of Beverly Innes throwing up on Barbie Patzweaver after tasting one of his dishes was a rather sour memory.

"We're investigators trying to find out what happened," she said. "I wonder if you saw an article in the *Tribune* implying that the Downhome Diner might have been behind what happened?"

Cyrus frowned. "Yes, I did. I thought drawing that kind of conclusion was irresponsible. I wrote to Mr. Prothro and told him as much."

"That's nice," Meredith said. "I'm sure it helped."

He shrugged. "I hope so, but regardless, I had to tell him what I thought about it."

"Mr. Sharrah," Julia began, "Jerome Matheson said the jar he put on the table contained paprika. He said you were the only person there when he dropped it off. We wondered if you noticed anything unusual. Did you see anyone tampering with it?"

He shook his head. "No. He told me to let the other contestants know that Ernie Prothro wanted us to use the paprika so that our dishes would have color." He shrugged. "I do that all the time, so it made sense to me. I didn't taste the paprika, because I trusted Ernie. He's interviewed us quite a few times on television. That's why it didn't concern me." He sighed. "To be honest, even though everyone knows there was something in that jar besides paprika, seeing poor Beverly Innes get sick all over Barbie Patzweaver after eating my food is a little hard to take. That's the last image I want in people's minds when they think about us."

"I can certainly understand that," Julia said, trying to hold back a desire to giggle.

"Is there anything you can tell us about that evening?" Meredith asked. "Something you might have noticed that could tell us what happened. How that ghost pepper got into the paprika jar?"

His eyes widened. "Ghost pepper? Is that what it was? The paper didn't say." He shook his head. "No wonder people got sick." He frowned. "If you mean did I see anyone fiddling with that jar, the answer is no." He shifted on his feet. "I wish I could assist you, but I can't think of anything I saw that would point you in the right direction. If I do…"

Meredith handed him a card. "Just give us a call."

"I will," he said, putting the card in his shirt pocket. "I don't use ghost pepper on any of my food. Too hot. Overpowers the flavor of the dish." He frowned. "I'm not sure I understand what the person responsible thought they were achieving. The contest was called off. No one was the winner. What was the point?"

"A question others have asked," Julia said. "We're still not sure why it was done, but we'd like to find the person behind it."

"Me too." Cyrus grimaced. "Still waiting for the jokes to stop." He smiled. "I'm not sure I helped you, but I'm glad I got to meet you all. Hope you enjoy your meals."

They thanked him before he walked away.

"Well, once again, we didn't learn anything," Meredith said. "Boy, Cyrus was surprised to hear ghost pepper was in that jar. I wonder…." She stopped talking and stared at Julia. "Are you okay?" she asked.

For a moment, Julia couldn't answer. Then she smiled at Meredith. "I know what happened," she said. "I know where the ghost pepper came from and who else was in on the robbery."

Chapter Thirty-Six

OFFICER FRETT SAT IN AN interrogation room with Meredith and Julia. Beau and Quin waited out in the hallway.

"Are you sure about this?" Officer Frett asked.

"As much as I can be," Julia said. "How long will it take Detective Akin to run that background check?"

"Not much longer."

The door to the room opened as Detective Akin, the detective who had been at Nora's house earlier in the day, walked in with a folder in her hand. She nodded at Julia and sat down at the table with them.

"You were right. It wasn't hard to verify," she said. "We also sent some people out to the location you suggested. We should hear from them soon. I suspect they'll confirm your suspicions. Our suspect is on his way here. He thinks we're just wrapping up our inquiries about the events at the contest."

"It was there in front of us the entire time," Meredith said. "We just missed it."

"I said this case was like a puzzle with some of the wrong pieces mixed in. But after Cyrus said what he did, I realized there was only one way it could have happened. After that, everything else fell into place."

"Well, I'm certain we'll soon have all the evidence we need to link Grady Prescott and our suspect together," Detective Akin said. "There's no way he can talk his way out of this."

Just then, someone knocked on the door. A young officer opened the door. "He's here," he said.

"Thank you, Miles," Detective Akin said. "Send him in."

A few moments later, the door opened and Jerome Matheson walked in. He looked surprised at all the people sitting around the table. "Nice to see you again," he said to Julia and Meredith. "I thought I would be talking to a detective about Friday night."

"You will be," Detective Akin said. "Have a seat."

Jerome sat down, a puzzled look on his face. "I don't understand...."

Detective Akin smiled. "Mrs. Foley, will you tell Mr. Matheson why we're here?" she asked.

"Certainly." Julia smiled at Jerome. "Tonight we were having dinner at Sharrah's on River Street. Cyrus was the only person involved with the grits contest we hadn't spoken to. He said something very interesting. Something we hadn't noticed before."

"I don't understand," Jerome said, frowning. "What does this have to do with me?"

"We were talking about the pepper sprinkled on the grits in the contest," Meredith said.

Jerome sighed. "This again? So what?"

"I mentioned to Cyrus that the jar was full of ghost pepper."

Jerome looked at her like she was crazy. "Yeah? So?"

"So," Julia said, "I mentioned to Cyrus that the jar of pepper accidentally used by the contestants was actually ground ghost pepper. He was surprised. He didn't know that. Then he mentioned that the newspaper had never shared just what kind of pepper was used."

Jerome's mustache started to quiver.

"I'm not sure if you know where this is going," Meredith said, "but Julia and I realized that no one we talked to knew what kind of pepper was in the bottle given to the contestants to use on their grits. No one except…you."

"That's right," Julia said. "I went back over my notes, and sure enough, you were the only person we talked to who referred to ground ghost pepper before we told them what kind it was. Now how did you know that?"

Jerome blew out a deep breath as if he'd been holding it in for a while. "That's it?" he asked, laughing. "You think you've captured a master criminal because I guessed what kind of pepper it was? I am a renowned chef, you know. *Ridicule*," he said loudly. "*Crétin!*"

"You can stop with the French phrases," the detective said. "We know you're not French."

"That's absurd," Jerome said.

"No, Norville, it's not," said Detective Akin.

The color suddenly drained from Jerome's face. Detective Akin opened the file in front of her. "Norville Muncton from Milledgeville, Georgia."

"How…I mean why—"

"Mrs. Foley and Mrs. Bellefontaine had an idea that you might have met Grady Prescott previously. Sure enough, we found that Norville Muncton met Prescott in prison. They were friends. Norville got out early for good behavior, changed his identity, and came to

Savannah, looking for a job. It seems Norville was a great cook. Had wanted to be a chef from an early age. But going to cooking school cost money his family didn't have. So, along with a friend, he stole what he needed from a bank in Milledgeville. He and the friend parted ways, and Norville finally went to cooking school in Atlanta. Changed his name. Graduated top of his class. Everything was going his way until his buddy in crime got caught during another robbery and gave Norville up so he could get a lighter sentence. So Norville went back to prison, where he hooked up with Grady again." The detective smiled. "How am I doing so far?" She closed the file. "I could go on, but here's the condensed version. After you got out, you changed your name once more. This time to Jerome Matheson. Then you applied for a job at Mama Louise's Kitchen. Told Laurel Hurst you came to Savannah because your daughter lives here. But you don't have a daughter. You came here because you thought you could get lost in the crowd. So many restaurants. You told Mrs. Hurst that the restaurant where you worked in Paris had burned down. You had a written letter of recommendation, but sadly, the owner of the restaurant had recently passed away in a terrible car accident. That was the truth. The restaurant really had burned down, and the owner had actually died. But she didn't write that letter. You never worked there a day in your life. But somehow you convinced Mrs. Hurst to hire you on a trial basis. Your cooking impressed her so much she decided to keep you."

"None of that is illegal," Norville said in clipped tones.

"Well, actually, using a fake identity is illegal, but it's nothing that would cause you any serious problems. All in all, things were going very well," Detective Akin said. "But then Prescott got out and looked you up. Not sure how he found you. You can fill us in on that later."

"Has Grady Prescott confirmed any of this nonsense?" Norville asked.

The detective shook her head. "Not yet."

Norville leaned back in his chair and crossed his arms, a smug smile on his face. "You're basing everything on this woman's lame accusation. I knew it was ghost pepper because I tasted it…after the incident."

"Oh, you tasted it all right," Julia said. "But it wasn't *after* the incident. It was before. At A Cup of Jo's. You set up an elaborate charade so it would look like the jar you brought to the contest really was paprika. But it wasn't. It was ground ghost peppers."

"Don't be ridiculous," he said. "I couldn't have just tasted ghost pepper and not had a violent reaction. No one could."

"You didn't," Julia said. "You tasted paprika at the coffee house, then brought an identical bottle to the contest, only it was filled with ground ghost pepper."

Julia fixed her gaze on the man she now saw as only a criminal. Not a great chef. "You wrote that letter yourself. Gave it to someone. Pretty sure it was Grady Prescott. He delivered it with the jar of paprika to the coffee shop. Then you came in on the day of the competition and put on your act. You took an identical jar, filled with ground ghost peppers, to the competition and convinced everyone that they needed to use *that* 'paprika' because it would make Ernie Prothro happy, and it would make their dishes look better on TV. But you didn't even need all of them to use it. Even one would give you what you needed, so you sprinkled a big dose on your own grits so the plan would work no matter what anyone else did. As long as you used it, one of the judges would get sick. As soon as the judges consumed the pepper, you called the police and told them someone had died and that several people had been poisoned. Grady was there to make sure the plan worked. Then he called Jerry and Shawn. Gave them the go-ahead for the coin shop. Everything worked beautifully. The police were so busy at the contest site that it took them longer to reach the coin shop after that call came in. Jerry and Shawn were gone by the time the police got there." She shook her head. "We suspected Grady Prescott, but we asked ourselves, how would he know Ernie Prothro or know that sometimes paprika is used to add color to certain dishes? It didn't make sense. Of course, the answer is that he was working with some-one who knew Ernie. And who knew food. You."

Norville laughed. "Pure conjecture. You have no proof for this outrageous fairy tale."

Just then Detective Akin's phone rang. She answered and listened for a moment before she said, "Thank you. I'll talk to you when you get here."

For the first time, Norville looked a little nervous. He didn't say anything, just stared at the detective.

She looked at Julia and Meredith. "You were right again."

"What are you talking about?" Norville asked, beads of sweat forming on his forehead.

"We just picked up Grady Prescott and two other men at your house," Detective Akin said. "Hiding in your basement. Prescott had the stolen coin and gave it to us." She gave Norville a slow smile. "Prescott is singing like a bird. Hoping he won't spend the rest of his life in prison if he cooperates."

"I want a lawyer," Norville shrieked. "Now. Call my attorney."

"Calm down and give me his name," Detective Akin said. "I'll call him right away." She looked at Meredith and Julia. "Let's step outside."

They got up and followed her out into the hall.

"You two delivered Mr. Muncton to us on a silver platter. Thank you. We'll take it from here."

"We're glad to hear that," Julia said with a sigh. "I'm going home to get a good night's sleep. Finally."

Meredith laughed. "I'm with you." She shook hands with the detective. "Thank you for everything you did. We'd love to get an update at some point, if you have the time."

"I'll find the time. Once again, thank you, ladies."

As the detective walked away, Julia smiled at Meredith. "I think we earned our fee for this one. After a good night's sleep, I think we need to collect our earnings. I'm thinking thinking about some Southern fried chicken, mashed potatoes with gravy, and the best collard greens in the city." She grinned at Meredith. "This will be the tastiest fee we've ever gotten."

Meredith laughed again as they walked out of the police station.

Chapter Thirty-Seven

June 1956

Clementine handed Granny Luv an old book. The covers were leather, but they were cracked and brittle like the pages inside.

"I realize it needs some care," Clementine said. "I'm sorry. I'm just not sure how to fix it."

"That doesn't matter, Clementine," Granny Luv said. "I'll take care of it." She frowned. "You said this is supposed to be passed down from one generation to another in your family. Don't you want to wait and give this to Luke?"

"I really want to take care of this now, Granny Luv. If Luke comes to you someday and asks for it, you can give it to him then. For now, I feel the right thing to do is to give it to you. I know you'll take care of it. Maybe someday, if Luke doesn't want it, you'll pass it down to Maggie Lu." Clementine sighed. "It must go to someone who will treasure it. Who understands how important it is."

"Why don't you sit down?" Granny Luv suggested. She was worried about her Clementine. She hadn't been well.

"Thank you." Clementine slipped into a chair.

Granny Luv put the tattered book on the table. "Coffee?" she asked.

Clementine nodded. Granny Luv noticed she'd grown much thinner. She'd always been so fragile. Granny Luv poured two cups of coffee, brought them to the table, and then sat down.

She gingerly opened the front cover of the book and carefully turned some of the pages. Inside were recipes written in longhand. The yellowed paper was brittle, and some of the edges were gone. She turned back to the first page. It was a note.

This cookbook was created by Bessie Goodman. The recipes belong to my mama, Portia Goodman. Mother Mathilda Beasley helped me put this all together. This book must be passed down through every generation. Mama says the recipes must stay in our family. Please make sure this happens. Mama was enslaved when she was younger. Her owners freed her and my father. I put this book together because I want everyone in our family to know that my mama is the greatest person I've ever known. She is strong, she is kind, and she works hard so that me and my brother can have the things she never had. My mama is more than a few recipes, but because there isn't anything else Black women can do right now, she became the best mother and wife she could be. The most important thing my mama taught us is that God loves us and has a plan for our lives that goes far beyond slavery or prejudice. Please use my mama's recipes and think of her when you do.

It was signed: Bessie Goodman, 1871.

Granny Luv blinked away tears. "Oh my," she said. "This is certainly special."

Clementine nodded. "It really is. There's also a letter." She reached into the pocket of her dress and pulled out an envelope. "It's not in great shape either. Bessie wrote it not long before she died. Like her mama, she wanted people to know who she was." Clementine smiled. "She became a teacher and affected the lives of many people. Her daughter, Maddie, became a nurse. Back then there were only a few Black doctors and no women doctors. She worked with a Dr. Samuel Bigsworthy, who trained her to work as a doctor even though she was never given the title. She was a great woman. Her brother, Theo, was a minister. He was a highly respected leader who taught his persecuted brothers and sisters to respond with love, not anger. He reminded them that it was God's job to punish evil and bring justice for the oppressed."

"Thank you," Granny Luv said. "I will take good care of this." It was obvious that giving her the book and the letter was extremely important to Clementine. She felt honored to have them and would make sure they continued to be shared down through generations of her family.

"There is one more thing," Clementine said. "I need to tell you about my parents, Sissie and Micah Jefferson. My father worked for the railroad and made a good living. They owned an acre of land, and my mother planted potatoes. She taught others to do the same so there would be food." She smiled. "My mother knew how to fix potatoes twenty

different ways. She helped to keep many hungry children fed. I was so proud of her." Suddenly her smile slipped, and her eyes filled with tears. *"When she was fifty-five, she caught a cold. My father told her to just rest. I was twenty years old and offered to take care of her. She wouldn't let me. She was afraid I'd catch her cold. She asked me to watch out for her potatoes and make sure families around us had plenty of them. I tried to do that, but I couldn't keep up. Thankfully, many in the community, people she'd helped, pitched in. We kept those potatoes growing."* She sighed. *"I had no idea how hard she worked until I tried to fill her shoes."* She took another deep breath. *"Her cold turned into pneumonia, and within days she was gone. Papa was away with the railroad when she died. We buried her about a week later."* Clementine looked into Granny Luv's eyes. *"Please tell Luke about my mother, Sissie Alvinia Jefferson. I want him to always know who she was."*

Granny Luv couldn't stop the tears that slipped down her cheeks. *"I promise. Everyone in my family will know about her...about all of them, from Portia on down."*

"Thank you."

Clementine finished her cup of coffee and stood to her feet. *"I've got to go lie down."* A look of contentment washed over her features. *"I've passed the cookbook and the stories down. I've done what I promised my mother I would do. I'm so relieved. Thank you again."*

"You're very welcome."

After Clementine went to her room, Granny Luv carefully turned each page of the book, gazing at the recipes. She planned to make every single one of them. Especially the shrimp and grits recipe. It looked delicious. She smiled to herself. She could hardly wait to show it to Maggie Lu. How that girl loved shrimp and grits. Granny Luv would also tell her the story of Portia and Bessie's family.

Chapter Thirty-Eight

Sunday after church the Downhome Diner was packed. Charlene led them to a table with a reserved sign on it. Once they were seated, Charlene said, "I need to check on Mirabelle. Rhonda's helping her today. So there's only Justine, Tara, and me to wait tables." She smiled. "Being too busy is a great problem to have. I'll be right back." She motioned to Justine. "Please get their drink orders," she said.

Justine nodded and smiled.

Julia was impressed by Charlene's calm reaction to the overflow of customers. But when she looked around, she noticed that everyone had a smile on their face. This wasn't just a busy restaurant, this was a gathering of friends. People really loved the diner and wanted to support it. They weren't worried about how long they would have to wait for a table or if their food took a little longer to get to them. They were just happy to be here.

A few minutes later, Julia saw Maggie Lu weaving her way through the busy restaurant, headed for their table.

"Isn't this wonderful?" she asked as she sat down. "Not sure what Ernie Prothro thought he was achieving by that snide remark in the paper, but it seems his influence doesn't amount to a hill of beans." She lowered her voice. "Frankly, that man's always been a little big for his britches." She laughed. "Charlene is so tickled with all the support, and she has you all and Jesus to thank for that."

"We're just happy it turned out this way," Meredith said. "Charlene's the one responsible though. If she hadn't worked so hard to make the Downhome Diner a successful restaurant, her customers wouldn't have come to her aid like this."

Maggie Lu stopped talking when Justine came to the table to take their drink orders. Once she walked away, Maggie Lu said, "Charlene says you have news for us. I take it you're waiting for her to join us?"

"Yes," Julia said. "We have a lot to tell you."

Maggie Lu's eyes widened. "You did it, didn't you? You know who snuck that hot pepper into the grits contest?" She grinned. "I knew you'd figure it out."

Charlene came over to the table and hugged her mother. Then she sat down next to Maggie Lu. "I'm ready," she said. "What did you want to tell me?"

"Last night the police arrested Jerome Matheson—excuse me, Norville Muncton."

Charlene looked at her with a puzzled expression. "I'm sorry, who?"

"Norville Muncton is Jerome's real name," Meredith said. "And he didn't come from Paris. He grew up in Milledgeville, Georgia."

Charlene blinked several times as if trying to digest this information. "I don't understand," she said finally. "Are you saying that Jerome is really this…Norville Muncton person?"

Julia nodded. "Exactly."

Charlene looked at her mother for a moment before she burst out laughing. "I can't believe it," she said, finally, wiping her eyes.

"I know," Julia said. "It was hard for us to believe too, but when we realized that Jerome was the only person who knew the pepper on the table at the competition was ghost pepper, it made us wonder about him. If there was a connection between the grits competition and the robbery, maybe Jerome and Prescott knew each other. A background check revealed Jerome's real identity. We have to credit Detective Akin for finding the information. It wasn't easy."

"So he never worked in Paris?" Maggie Lu asked.

Julia shook her head. "No. But he knew about a very successful restaurant in Paris that burned down years ago. Not long before he came to Savannah, the owner was killed in a terrible car wreck. So Jerome, I mean Norville Muncton, forged a letter of recommendation from her. Once he cooked for Laurel Hurst she bought his lies hook, line, and sinker. He became Chef Jerome Matheson."

Justine came up to the table with their drinks. She asked if they were ready to order, but Charlene said, "Give us a few minutes, Justine. I'll let you know."

Justine nodded and walked away.

"Keep going," Charlene said.

After taking a drink of her Diet Dr Pepper, Julia told them the rest of it, including how Jerome switched the jars, how Grady made the police think Julia was harassing him, and about the confrontation with Grady at Nora's house.

"So where is Muncton now?" Quin asked. "And Prescott?"

"Both in jail," Julia said. "Each trying to blame the other."

"How did the police find them?" Charlene asked.

"They called Muncton down to the station to question him. And while they were doing that, they got a warrant to search his house. Prescott, Muncton, and two of Prescott's friends, the men who actually held up the coin store, were all hiding there. Waiting to sell the coin to the black market buyer who was going to pay them a fortune. They thought they were safe at Muncton's house because no one had tied Prescott and Muncton together. They figured that if that ever happened, they'd be long gone."

"They didn't know who they were up against," Beau said with a smile. "Two of the best investigators in Savannah."

Julia smiled at him. "Thanks, dear."

"Crystal, the young woman who works at the coin shop, is also testifying against Prescott and his friends," Meredith said. "The police are convinced she had nothing to do with setting up the robbery. She just trusted the wrong person with information he used against her."

"Will she keep her job?" Maggie Lu asked.

Julia nodded. "And I think she's finally noticed a special young man who works there. The right kind of man. I hope something good comes out of it."

"What about the coin?" Charlene asked. "Did they find it?"

Julia smiled. "Yes, they did. So in the end, everything turned out just as it should." She gazed around the restaurant. "Maybe the True Grits contest didn't bring in customers the way you planned," she said to Charlene, "but regardless, here they are. I hope your business continues to grow."

"I hope so too," Charlene said. She motioned to Justine, who was a couple of tables away. "And now, we order. Lunch is on me," she said. "You've earned it…and more."

"This time we'll accept it," Meredith said with a smile. "Thank you, Charlene."

"You're welcome. Now, if you'll excuse me, I need to see if Maribelle needs any help. But I'll be back."

Justine came up to the table just as Charlene walked away. After they'd ordered, Maggie Lu said, "I have something to show you all." She reached into the satchel she'd brought with her and took out something wrapped in plastic.

"I know what this is," Julia said. "It's the cookbook."

"Yes'm, it is." Maggie Lu put the plastic-wrapped book on the table and carefully removed it from the bag that held it. It had dark blue leather covers that showed its years, but it had been restored and seemed to be in excellent shape. Maggie Lu carefully opened the front cover. "This book was written by Bessie Goodman Evans, a Black woman who became a teacher in the early years of Savannah. I know I told you her story and the story of her mama, Portia Goodman. But if it's okay with you, while we're waiting for our food, I'd like to also tell you the story of Bessie's daughter, Maddie, and her daughter, Sissie. And then I'd like to tell you about the woman who gave this book to my grandmother. Clementine Jefferson Clement, my sister-in-law. I intend to write everything down as it was told to Granny Luv and add it to this collection. That way these remarkable ladies will live for a long, long time in the memories of their families." She smiled at the group assembled at the table. "All of you certainly qualify as family."

Julia reached over and took her precious friend's hand. "Maggie Lu, it would be an honor to hear about them." She looked at Meredith, who nodded and returned her partner's smile.

Dear Reader,

Savannah has a rich history, but there is also heartbreak and injustice in its past. Savannah's founder, James Oglethorpe, stood against people enslaving other people, but when his influence was gone, slavery flourished. Yet even in the middle of iniquity, heroes stood out. I included one of them in *True Grits*. Mother Mathilda Beasley brought enslaved people into her home and educated them even though it was against the law. If she'd been caught, she would have had to pay a stiff fine and receive up to thirty-two lashes in the public square. There were several others also committed to teaching enslaved Blacks to read and write, but to the credit of the citizens of Savannah, most people looked the other way.

In *True Grits*, I introduce Portia Goodman and her daughter, Bessie. Portia is a free woman, living with her husband, Cletus, Bessie, and Bessie's brother, Joseph. They are one of few families who received even a portion of the "40 Acres and a Mule" promised to freed slaves during Reconstruction.

I hope you've enjoyed the twists and turns of a new mystery and being on the case again with Meredith and Julia of Magnolia Investigations!

God bless you,
Nancy Mehl

About the Author

Nancy Mehl is a *USA Today* bestselling author. She's been a finalist for the Carol Award three times and won the award once. She was a finalist for two Reviewers' Choice Awards from RT Book Reviews and was also nominated for the coveted Christy Award.

Book three in her Kaely Quinn Profiler series, *Dead End*, was released in March 2020. The first book in Nancy's new series, *Night Fall*, part of the Quantico Files, is available as of 2021.

Nancy lives in Missouri with her husband, Norman, and their Puggle, Watson. Readers can learn more about Nancy through her Web site: nancymehl.com. She is part of the Suspense Sisters: suspensesisters.blogspot.com, along with several other popular suspense authors. She is also a member of the BOLO Squad on Facebook, a private group with some of today's best-loved suspense authors.

The Truth Behind the Fiction

Mother Mathilda Beasley

MATHILDE (LATER CHANGED TO MATHILDA) Taylor was born in New Orleans in 1832. Her mother was enslaved, and her father was probably Native American.

As a young woman, Mathilda moved to Savannah as a free person of color. In 1860, the city census listed 705 free Black citizens. Free people had rights and privileges enslaved people didn't; however, they were forced to wear a badge indicating their status.

That same census lists Mathilda Taylor as a seamstress. She sewed to support herself, but her main goal was to teach Black children how to read, write, and do math. Even though these schools were an "open secret," students had to hide their books from the authorities. They wrapped them in newspapers or put them in baskets covered with the kind of wood chips many poor people used for fuel.

In 1869 Mathilda married Abraham Beasley, a successful Black businessman. After his death in 1877, Mathilda went to York, England, to study as a nun. In 1886 she returned to Savannah and started an orphanage. In 1889, Mathilda founded the first group of Black nuns in Georgia. Under her direction, they kept the orphanage going for several years. In 1899 she took the habit of the Franciscans and continued working at her beloved orphanage. In 1901, Mathilda was given a cottage near the Sacred Heart Church to which she had earlier given her husband's landholdings. She began to sew in her home and give the proceeds to disadvantaged Black people. On December 20, 1903, the much beloved "Mother Beasley" was found dead kneeling in the cottage's private chapel. Nearby were her burial clothes, funeral instructions, and will.

SOMETHING DELICIOUS FROM A
Downhome Southern Kitchen

PORTIA'S SHRIMP AND GRITS

Ingredients:

4 cups chicken broth

½ teaspoon salt

¼ teaspoon pepper (white pepper okay)

1 cup stone-ground grits

4 tablespoons butter

4 slices bacon, chopped

1 tablespoon smoked paprika (You can buy this or make your own. Directions below.)

1 pound shrimp, peeled and deveined

1 clove garlic, minced

1 stalk celery, thinly sliced

1 tablespoon lemon juice

2 tablespoons chopped parsley

1 cup thinly sliced scallions

Instructions:

Bring broth, salt, and pepper to boil in large pot before adding grits and butter, stirring and cooking for 20 to 22 minutes or until liquid is gone.

Add bacon to skillet and cook until crisp, then remove from pan and add shrimp and smoked paprika seasoning. Cook shrimp for 1 to 2 minutes on each side.

Remove cooked shrimp and add garlic, celery, and lemon juice. Cook for 1 minute before adding shrimp and bacon to pan and stirring to combine.

Serve shrimp mixture over grits and garnish with parsley, scallions, and light dusting of smoked paprika.

RECIPE FOR SMOKED PAPRIKA

Ingredients:

   1 (3 ½ ounce) bottle liquid smoke, hickory
   1 (18 ounce) bottle Spanish paprika

Instructions:

In a large bowl slowly whisk ingredients together. Once lumps are gone, spread out on foil-lined cookie sheet to dry overnight.

*Read on for a sneak peek of another exciting book
in the Savannah Secrets series!*

Sapphire Secret
BY MARLENE CHASE

MEREDITH BELLEFONTAINE RAN A HAND through her short blond curls, which the sun turned to warm silk against her fingers. She made the short jaunt to Magnolia Investigations, buoyed with enthusiasm. It was a new day. A new week. Anything could happen.

In the eighteen months since she'd reopened her husband's agency, a lot of water had flowed down the Savannah River. Like the river, which was sometimes wild and dangerous and sometimes benign as a doting mother's smile, days had never been dull.

She sighed happily as she joined Julia in the agency's parking area behind Whitaker Street. "On a day like this, you can't think of November as bleak or cold like some fierce prophet, warning of winter. Magnolias are still blooming, and even this early in the morning I hardly need this jacket."

Julia Foley rolled expressive gray eyes at her best friend and partner as they lingered by their cars. She smiled. "That's why our fair city is so full of festivals and art fairs—and marathons this time of the year. And you, Mrs. Bellefontaine, look ready to run one—a marathon, that is."

Meredith returned the smile. She and Julia had arrived for work at the same time, but neither seemed anxious to go inside. Julia's long arms were crossed over her forest-green suit jacket that contrasted perfectly with her silver hair. Tall and formidable, whether in a judge's robe or dressed for a day at the office, she looked every bit the sharp-minded and adventurous woman that she was.

They had met in college and become fast friends. Then life had swept them along in divergent currents until they discovered each other again. Meredith blessed the day she had convinced the former juvenile court judge of Chatham County to join her at Magnolia Investigations. She had surprised even herself when, after Ron's death, she decided to reopen the business which he had so conscientiously built up.

"Well, I don't think I'm ready for a marathon," Meredith said, "but there's no denying that this is one gorgeous Savannah day. November is one of my favorite months. And Thanksgiving will be here before we know it."

Julia followed her gaze, glancing up at the sun that gilded the tops of trees. A nearby strip of woods had been preserved in the historic district amid stately homes and office buildings. "You're right," she said. "November in Savannah has plenty of warmth for comfort and just enough briskness to energize a person."

Meredith breathed in the freshness of the morning. Not knowing what the day would hold was part of its mystique, but there was a certain knowing, an awareness that "the mercies of the Lord were new every morning." She let out a big breath. "I'm not sure I'd survive a marathon, but an easy stroll in the park would be tempting on a day like this. What do you think?"

"I won't be running any marathons today either," Julia said with a groan. "I spent Saturday taking some of the youth from church on a hike at Skidaway Park. You've no idea how twenty-two junior high kids can wear a body down."

Julia was a high-energy gal who thrived on hard-hitting action and solving dilemmas. Only her critical thinking skills kept her from jumping into something with both feet before she put on her shoes.

"But it's Monday," she said with resignation. "And somebody's got to open the office. Carmen's not coming in until ten this morning, remember?"

"That's right." Carmen had said she needed to keep an important appointment for Harmony, the little girl she mentored from the Boys and Girls Club. Their assistant, who had struggled growing up, was now encouraging others.

"Stars and garters! What do you make of that?"

Meredith spun around at Julia's exclamation.

A young woman—a teenager, perhaps—was running their way. Her feet barely touched the ground as she sprinted toward them. She was thin as an arrow, wearing jeans and a white shirt. Blond hair bobbed behind her and drizzled around her face as she came closer. Her breath came in quick, short gasps.

Meredith stared as she kept coming, not slowing down at all. Would she run straight into them? The girl's eyes flashed, scanning the parking lot and buildings as she advanced on soundless feet.

"Good heavenly days!" Julia muttered, lurching forward.

And then the girl stopped inches away. "Miss Bellefontaine?" she panted in a high-pitched voice that was childlike and urgent. Deep blue eyes—nearly black—flashed, oddly discordant with her light skin and hair.

"I'm Meredith Bellefontaine," Meredith said. "Can I help you?"

"Please!" She clasped small hands at the bare spot between her shirt and jeans and bent over to catch her breath. "I—I need your help. And—and I can pay you!" The disturbing eyes flashed left and right, then over her shoulder.

Meredith scrambled through her memory. Did she know this girl who seemed to know who she was? A waitress from one of the cafés in the area? Maybe she was a retail worker from one of the shops nearby. She searched the heart-shaped face, which was very pale, making her eyes pop like black marbles. Her small chin trembled slightly. There was a small design on the pocket of her white shirt, which appeared to have been hastily tied at her waist.

"What's wrong?" Meredith asked. "How can we help you?"

"Please! I can't talk long. I have to get back, but I have to find out why—" She froze suddenly and then jerked her head to the left. Her mouth formed a startled O. "Someone is following me!"

Meredith scanned the area but saw no one. It was not yet eight thirty in the morning, and the parking lot was deserted. "Who? Who is following you?" she urged. She took a step toward the young woman, who quickly backed up like a skittish cat, flashing those glistening eyes around the parking area yet again.

Julia too went toward her, hands outstretched. "Try to calm down. No one can hurt you here."

She shook her head violently, locked eyes with Meredith. "I need to hire you. I've got to know. Please!"

Know who was following her, Meredith supposed, scanning the area but seeing no one. "Calm down and tell us what's wrong."

Her head bobbed again—left, right, before focusing once more on Meredith. "I can pay you!" She reached into the pocket of trendy designer jeans, fished out a wad of bills, and thrust them into Meredith's hand.

"Wait!" Meredith said, closing her fingers over the bills before they could spill onto the ground. "Our office is right behind us." She gestured with her free hand. "Why don't we go inside and talk—"

"I can't right now!" came the abrupt refusal. The young woman shifted from side to side in a quick rocking motion, her canvas shoes making no sound. The dark eyes flashed. "I have to get back! Please...I have to go!"

Meredith took a sustaining breath. "Go where? Who are you? How do you know us?"

The young woman looked behind her frantically, then reached up to push strands of damp hair from her forehead. "I—I know who you are. My grandma—"

A crack in the bushes several yards to their left brought a startled gasp to her pale lips. Before Meredith or Julia could react, she bolted like a frightened gazelle. She streaked away in the opposite direction from the sound, her hair streaming behind her like a tattered flag in the wind.

"Wait!" Meredith yelled as Julia took off in the direction of the bushes.

The young woman fled around to the front of the building. Meredith ran after her, chasing her onto Whitaker and then into Forsyth Park, but her heels were no match for the fleet-footed young woman's sneakers. Meredith ran for several yards without catching sight of her. Likely she had detoured into the brush, but in what direction?

Besides, there were thirty acres of walking trails in the famous park. People were taking advantage of the lovely green space still fragrant with late-autumn flowers.

Breathing hard, Meredith stopped, the money still clutched in her hand. She crammed it into her purse. There was no point in trying to catch the girl, so with an embarrassed shrug for the curious watchers, she headed back the way she had come. The fleeing young woman would return—if for no other reason than to claim her money.

"I couldn't catch her," she gasped upon rejoining Julia in the parking lot. "You see anything?"

"Someone was there all right," Julia said, brows drawn together in a silver line. "He went racing through that strip of woods and disappeared. Unfortunately, there are plenty of buildings to sneak into and back gardens to hide in. All I got was a glimpse of two skinny legs and a pair of cowboy boots."

Meredith held her aching side. "So much for my marathon readiness," she gasped. "Let's get inside. I need a drink of water."

Julia opened the door to the agency's rear entrance. Meredith veered to the right and stepped into the warm kitchen with its comforting gray walls. She dropped her purse on the island counter and pulled a glass from the cupboard.

"Who do you think she was?" Julia asked, nearly knocking over the vase of orange mums Carmen had brought in on Friday.

"I've never seen her before," Meredith said after a restoring gulp of water. "I've been racking my brain, trying to think of some connection we might have had." Meredith felt a tightening in her chest. What was happening to the young woman? "She was just a girl, Julia. What would you say? Seventeen, eighteen?"

Julia pulled a glass down for herself. "Maybe," she mumbled, "but there was something about her eyes—like maybe she had seen a lot more than high school." She frowned. "I don't know, but she was sure scared out of her wits. Wish I could have caught that guy— whoever he was."

"She was really frightened—almost hysterical," Meredith murmured. At least whoever the young woman thought was following her had fled in the opposite direction and not gone after her. The large eyes in the heart-shaped face burrowed into Meredith's mind, engraving their dark pathos there. Her heart lurched as she recalled the desperate plea for help. Why hadn't the young woman gone to the police instead of running to the first stranger she thought might help her?

"I know who you are," she had said. Meredith chewed the inside of her cheek. No, she hadn't come to a stranger. She had come to someone she knew—or knew of. And what was that about a grandma? Meredith searched her mind for any tie that made sense.

"She came prepared to pay for help," Julia said, breaking into Meredith's scattered thoughts.

"Yes! The money!" Meredith scrambled to open her purse and retrieve the wad she had stashed there when the girl had bolted out of sight. She folded out the roll, saw a hundred-dollar bill on top. Where had a teenager come up with that kind of money? She began thumbing through the notes with growing amazement.

"Those are hundred-dollar bills!" Julia exclaimed.

Meredith caught her partner's startled gaze. "Yes. Every one of them. Jules, there's a thousand dollars here."

"Where would a kid like that get a thousand bucks? Do you suppose that's what the guy in the bushes was after?"

Meredith shook her head, unable to articulate her own surprise. She'd expected a few sweaty tens in the crumpled wad, but a thousand dollars! The frightened young woman had left it behind. It made no sense at all.

Julia released a long breath. "Surely she'll be back. She's not about to let all this money get away with nothing to show for it."

What if she can't get back? Whoever was lurking in the bushes had run away in the opposite direction. He hadn't gone after her. But suppose he did later?

"I wonder why she ran. Whoever was following her wouldn't have tried anything right in front of our agency," Julia said. "But we'd better report it." Julia punched in some numbers on her phone and described the young woman who had come out of nowhere asking for help and then run away.

Julia told the dispatcher of her unsuccessful attempt to catch the man wearing cowboy boots. No, they had no idea who he was or who the young woman was. "They'll send someone to patrol the area," she said after ending the call and tucking her cell phone away, "but I don't really expect anything will come of it."

Meredith set her water glass down. She looked up at Julia, who was twirling a strand of hair around her ear. "What do you think we should do now?"

Julia raised her eyebrows and let the strand of hair fall away. "Just wait, I suppose. Surely she'll be back to claim her thousand bucks. I bet she won't let much grass grow under her feet either."

Meredith nodded. There was little else they could do for the moment. They had no idea where to find her—or how to keep her safe. She drew in a sharp breath, haunted by the small pale face. So young, so vulnerable. Kinsley a few years hence perhaps. What—or who—was she running from? And how could they help her?

As she headed for her office, another ripple of concern marred the bright November day. Something was going on with her own sweet granddaughter, Kinsley Faith. She hadn't been her usual chatty self during their last virtual get-together. She'd been temperamental and pouty. She had even moved away from the camera, causing her mother to gently rebuke her for not paying the proper attention to Gran.

Kinsley was usually ready with a dramatic catalog of her activities. She'd been a girly-girl from the beginning. It was such fun to find the perfect pink dress or a new animal figurine for her collection. It was lovely to have a little girl to love. Of course, Kinsley's interests were changing. Gran would have to be sensitive to them—and perhaps to new moods and reactions.

Carter's two children, Kinsley and her brother, Kaden, were growing up so fast, but every mother and grandmother felt that way, didn't they? Kaden, eleven going on Einstein, loved all things science—especially astronomy. Meredith had been itching to give him a real hug—not a virtual one. Kaden's Asberger's syndrome kept him wary of close contact—even hers.

What would they be like later, when they were the age of the frightened young woman who had split the morning? And if they were in trouble—heaven forbid—who would reach out to them with a loving hand?

She whispered a prayer that God who witnessed the tiny sparrow's fall would keep His eye on the children of this world, especially the frightened young woman who had run to them for help.

A Note from the Editors

WE HOPE YOU ENJOY THE Savannah Secrets series, created by the Books and Inspirational Media Division of Guideposts, a nonprofit organization that touches millions of lives every day through products and services that inspire, encourage, help you grow in your faith, and celebrate God's love in every aspect of your daily life.

Thank you for making a difference with your purchase of this book, which helps fund our many outreach programs to military personnel, prisons, hospitals, nursing homes, and educational institutions. To learn more, visit GuidepostsFoundation.org.

We also maintain many useful and uplifting online resources. Visit Guideposts.org to read true stories of hope and inspiration, access OurPrayer network, sign up for free newsletters, download free e-books, join our Facebook community, and follow our stimulating blogs.

To learn about other Guideposts publications, including the bestselling devotional *Daily Guideposts*, go to ShopGuideposts.org, call (800) 932-2145, or write to Guideposts, PO Box 5815, Harlan, Iowa 51593.